Christine's Odyssey

Book 1 Simms Sibling Series
by
J.L. Campbell

Christine's Odyssey
Copyright © 2013 J.L. Campbell
Published by The Writers' Suite

This is a work of fiction. References to events, characters, organizations and places are fictional and the product of the author's imagination. Any similarity to actual events and people living or dead is coincidental.

ISBN 13: 978-976-95586-0-1
ISBN 10: 9769558605

For the voiceless ones in our society.

Chapter 1

A scream woke Christine.

Then a series of thuds and bumps forced her upright in bed.

Her heart fluttered against her ribs and she put a hand to her chest, waiting for her breathing to go back to normal.

In the gloom, another bang startled her. She rubbed her arms to keep the chill away and pulled the sheet around her shoulders, cocking her head toward the door.

What was it this time?

Her father's soothing voice reached her ears, his words unclear. He was reasoning with her mother. As usual.

A familiar heaviness settled in her chest and swelled to block her throat.

Saturday had erupted in the Simms' household.

Cassandra snorted and flung a hand over Jamielle, who twitched and dug Christine with an elbow.

Another round of crashes and thumps invaded the bedroom. Both girls stirred, and seven-year-old Cassandra sat up and rubbed her eyes. "What's that?"

"Ma'am and Daddy are fighting again," Christine said.

"Oh." Cass lay down and snuggled against Jamielle, who snuffled into her pillow.

Nothing ever changed at their house—the constant quarrels, her mother losing her temper and breaking things, her father trying to keep the peace.

Not for the first time, Christine wondered why she wasn't born in a different family; one that lived in Kingston or even in the next parish, Manchester. Another island would be better. Maybe Antigua or Cayman, places she had learned about in Social Studies.

Instead, their family didn't have much, and lived deep in the St. Elizabeth bush lands of Jamaica.

Shutting her wishful thoughts away, Christine threw back the blanket. She shivered when cold air bit her skin through her nightgown. The wooden floor groaned as she crossed to the dresser in the corner. She got her clothes and moved to the door, cringing at the banging of pots and pans on the stovetop. Before she crept into the passage, she glanced toward the kitchen.

Ma'am wasn't in sight. Good.

She tiptoed toward the bathroom, wincing when the hinges on the bedroom door creaked. In the stillness, it was as loud as the rooster that bellowed across the yard at daybreak.

"Chris?"

Her mother's voice stopped her, and Christine scraped her bottom lip with her teeth, wondering what she'd done this time. When she heard her name a second time, Christine answered, keeping her fingers crossed for good luck. Not that it worked most times.

"It's about time you got up," Ma'am said. "Come here."

Christine sighed and her shoulders drooped. She focused on her feet as she entered the kitchen, knowing better than to provoke her mother, who would interpret a direct look as a challenge.

The smell of cabbage made Christine's stomach twist. *That's the third time this week.*

They always ate food that came out of a can. Otherwise, they ate cabbage. Mommy, or Ma'am as Christine preferred to call her, never prepared anything else.

Christine paid attention when Ma'am spat angry words. "You think I'm here to clean up after you?"

Although Ma'am had asked a question, Christine didn't give an answer because her mother didn't expect one.

"Next time I find anythin' left in the sink overnight, I'm gonna slap you silly."

Christine looked up through her lashes as Ma'am's mouth twisted in a sneer. "You might be your Daddy's princess, but to me you're just another mouth to feed, not to mention more work."

Christine stared at her toes, hoping for a quick escape. She raised her head when Ma'am stabbed the air between them with a finger. "You hearin' me?"

Christine nodded and braced herself.

The whack across the side of her face made her eyes and nose water. Ma'am's rant wouldn't be complete without a slap. Glaring at Christine, Ma'am pressed her forehead and then closed her eyes. "Go bathe and start tidyin' the house."

Christine turned away, holding back tears. It didn't matter that *she* hadn't left any plates in the sink. Ma'am would have slapped her anyway. She shut the bathroom door and approached the chipped basin. In the mirror, she expected to see a bruise at the side of her face, but nothing marred her skin.

Her two pigtails curled at the ends and her brown eyes gazed back through the spots in the glass. She grabbed the unruly plaits and held them to her ears, but they kicked up in the air when she released them. To take her mind off the latest slap, Christine wriggled her eyebrows, which made her break into a smile.

She turned on the brass tap and started her morning routine. The repetitive movements while brushing her teeth were comforting, putting her into a near trance. When she finished, Christine rinsed her mouth, looked at her teeth and stuck her tongue out to examine it before she was satisfied. Into the chipped enamel cup her toothbrush went, along with six others that leaned in different directions.

Her least favourite part came next. She yanked off her nightdress and hopped into the shower, turning on the pipe before she could change her mind. The water from the underground tank was always cold. She soaped and rinsed herself, then scampered out of the stall, shivering the entire time.

"Chris!"

The shout jolted Christine, and when her feet settled on the cracked tiles, she yelled back, "Yes, Ma'am?"

"What you doin' in there so long?"

"I'm almost finished."

"Hurry up!"

Christine gathered her things and went back to the bedroom. At the sound of the door closing, Cassandra stirred, and settled closer to Jamielle.

In front of the mirror, Christine loosed her hair and neatened her two plaits before opening the window. The sun's rays came through the lace curtains, showing the nicks and scratches in the old furniture. Her sisters squirmed when sunlight flooded their space.

Christine avoided looking anywhere in their bedroom. Outside the window, droplets of dew winked and sparkled, welcoming the new day. The chickens scratched and pecked through the dirt and grass hunting for food, while the family's two puppies bit and rolled over each other in their usual game. The doors of the shed where her father stored his tools yawned open. At this time of the morning, Daddy would be inside cleaning and oiling the equipment he used on the farm.

She looked up at the John Crow mountains, as she did every day. Ever since she could remember, she dreamed of what lay beyond their misty peaks.

She fantasized about the people who lived on the other side. What did they do? How did they live? Perhaps, an eleven-year-old girl like herself was over there thinking about the same things. Christine lived for this moment each morning, when she forgot her life for a few minutes and lost herself in daydreams.

"Christine!"

This time, her name was a scream. She hurried to the bed and shook Cassandra. The door crashed against the wall and Ma'am stood in the doorway.

"I'm w-waking the girls," Christine said.

"Well, get them up, bathed and dressed. Now. I don't understan' why it takes you three times longer to do anythin' than a normal person."

She left, muttering to herself, a cigarette pressed between her thumb and forefinger. The nasty odor of the smoke tickled Christine's nostrils, making her want to sneeze.

While Cassandra stretched, Christine coaxed Jamielle out of sleep, but she snuggled deeper into her pillow.

Cassandra leaned over their five-year-old sister. "I know how to wake her!"

She poked Jamielle's side, but she squirmed and didn't open her eyes. Cassandra continued tickling Jamielle, who lashed out with her leg. The kick caught Cassandra in the face. She screamed and covered her nose with both hands. Blood trickled through her fingers, and tears came to her eyes.

Ma'am rushed down the hallway, cursing. The door opened and she raced into the room with a rubber flip-flop in one hand. "I swear before the day is out I'm gonna knock one of you into next week! What the hell is happenin' in here, Christine?"

Without waiting for an answer, Ma'am came to the side of the bed where Christine sat. She scampered off the bed, but not fast enough. The neck of her tee-shirt tore when Ma'am grabbed it.

Christine put a hand up to ward off the slaps she knew were coming. Her luck had run out and the day had just started.

Chapter 2

The blows set Christine's arm on fire, but she held it up to protect her face. Cassandra and Jamielle begged Ma'am to let her go, but their cries didn't help.

Christine saw herself in her mother's grip, as though standing in one corner of the room and watching parts of a movie she'd seen many times. Her mother's skinny body looked like that of an old woman, but the force behind the blows felt as if she had superhuman strength.

Christine lowered her hand, which now trembled and burned as if fire ants had run loose on her skin. The slipper caught her between the eyes, blinding her for a few seconds.

Ma'am let her go and she stumbled, grabbing at the air. With one hand, Christine wiped her eyes and used the other to hold her shirt together. She steadied herself, still puzzled as to why Ma'am had released her.

The rumble of Daddy's voice helped Christine figure out what had happened. He had grabbed Ma'am by the arm, moved her toward the door and forced her out of the room. They argued on the way down the passage, and a door slammed.

Christine slumped on the bed where her sisters sat sniffling and wiping their eyes. After her heart stopped pumping and she wasn't sweating so much, Christine pulled a shirt out of the dresser drawer to swap with the one she wore. She avoided looking at herself in the mirror and leaned against the wall, her head bowed.

The unfairness of everything got to her and she slid down and settled on the floor, sobbing while she hugged her knees and rocked herself. Cass and Jamie crouched on both sides of her, stroking her hair, but she didn't acknowledge them. They cried with her as they always did.

When her tears stopped, Christine changed her shirt and went to the bathroom with her sisters trailing behind her. She splashed water over her face, dried it with a towel and then cleaned the blood off Cassandra's hands and face. She had a split lip and a nosebleed. Christine made Cassandra tip her head back, and stuffed a bit of tissue in her nostril to catch the blood.

After helping them bathe, Christine lay across the bed with the two younger girls curled against her. She stared out the window, chin resting on top of her folded hands. Then she examined the patterns the welts made on her arm and decided to talk to Daddy about something she had been thinking over for a long time. Today was as good a day as any to speak to him.

She got off the bed, and Cass and Jamielle followed. On the way past their parents' door, Daddy's voice drifted to Christine. "...every time we argue, you take it out on Christine. I only have to disappear for five minutes for you to start abusing her."

Christine's footsteps slowed and then stopped.

Her father continued, "Christine is not the problem. Neither am I. You are the problem, Ellen. You're spiteful and selfish and you've gone back on your word. You promised to take care of her..."

His voice faded and started up closer to where Christine stood. "...all you care about is yourself. You wanted to be a mother. Well, you *are* one five times over, so grow up and act like it!"

The door opened and Christine came face to face with her father. She had never seen him angrier—lips clamped together and eyebrows rumpled in a frown. He said nothing, but squeezed her shoulder on his way toward the kitchen and out the back door.

Those words were the most Christine had heard him say to her mother in weeks. Most times, Ma'am talked non-stop, and he refused to answer. Her spirit sank further when glass splintered in her parents' room.

Christine went to the kitchen, where she laid out seven place mats and cutlery and then sat waiting. She tuned out her sisters' chatter by counting the rust marks on the fridge. Daddy called them iron mould.

The sound of rushing feet warned Christine that Sam, her nine-year-old brother, was running through the hall again. Most likely, he was chasing Josh, the baby of the family. Josh proved her right when he toddled into the kitchen and waggled his hands at her. It was his way of asking to be picked up.

"Kwistee." He gurgled her name, and she lifted him to sit on her lap.

Sam raced in behind Josh, saw that he was occupied, and took his seat. "Morning."

Cassandra and Jamielle answered him and then continued their conversation.

When Ma'am's slippers flapped toward them, everybody stopped talking. Christine pulled out the seat next to Sam, sat Josh in it, and dropped into her chair. Ma'am grunted at them and crossed to the cupboards.

The back door opened and Daddy came inside and took his seat. His gaze rested on each of them, but a bit longer on Christine, especially her arm. "Everybody all right?"

They nodded, smiling at him.

Ma'am turned with the plates in hand and their smiles faded.

On Saturday mornings, the family ate together. Out of habit, the girls sat on one side of the table. The boys sat on the other and Ma'am and Daddy faced each other. They ate in silence, except for the clanging of knives and forks against their plates.

Christine tried not to screw her face up while she forced boiled, green bananas and steamed cabbage down her throat. She disliked the smell, and to make things worse, Ma'am always made it soggy. Bits of shrivelled tomatoes and droopy thyme stared back at her. She glanced at Josh's plate. At least he got his bananas crushed with butter.

He sat on a cushion in the chair next to Ma'am, who spooned food into his mouth, although he wanted to feed himself. The moment they finished eating, Sam, Cassandra and Jamielle excused themselves and ran out to the back yard. Josh slid off his chair and staggered behind them.

"Try not to get dirty like a hog foot rope, and keep an eye on Josh!" Ma'am yelled.

Christine cleared away the things her brothers and sisters had used, gripping the plates tight to stop them from clattering. She had removed almost everything and stood cleaning the mats, when Ma'am spoke. "I'm done. You can take these things."

Christine edged toward her and picked up the plate. When she reached for the cup, Ma'am snapped, "Have some manners. Don't stretch over me."

To stop the cutlery from rattling, Christine held them tight and walked around to Ma'am's other side.

Christine picked up the cup, and tea sloshed over the rim, wetting the place mat.

Ma'am glared at her. "You're so clumsy. Only God knows how you don't break everythin' you touch."

Out of the corners of her eyes, Christine looked at Daddy. He shook his head and laid both hands on the table. "Would you give her a break?"

Ma'am didn't say anything, but cut her eyes at Christine.

Christine knew Daddy felt her pain and understood her better than anyone else. He must have been upset over what happened earlier because he normally wouldn't say anything that might cause another beating when he left the house.

Love for him warmed her whole body. Sometimes, she wished Ma'am would die or go away and never come back, so their lives would be happy.

Her brothers' and sisters' yells cut into her thoughts, and something invisible, but heavy fell on Christine's chest. She had never been allowed to laugh, run and play because Ma'am expected her to do all the housework.

Fresh tears scorched Christine's eyes. She wanted to be anywhere else but home. The need to speak to Daddy alone burned her insides.

She'd talk to him on their trip to town later in the day.

Chapter 3

Christine turned her face up to the sun, enjoying the heat on her skin. Behind the barbed wire fencing on both sides of the road, a light breeze shifted the waist-high Guinea grass. Daddy squeezed her hand and she looked up at him.

"You okay?" he asked.

She nodded and returned the squeeze. "I'm thinking about which books I should get this trip. Maybe something that Sam will like too, maybe a Hardy Boys adventure."

"As long as you're both learning from what you're reading, I don't mind. Mrs. King can help you choose something."

"Nah, I prefer to search until I find exactly what I want."

He switched the books they were returning to the library from one arm to the next, and moved into the shade. "No problem, but remember…"

Christine helped Daddy to finish the sentence. "Nothing below my comprehension level."

The trip into Clarkesville formed the high point of each week. Everything was right in her world then. Whenever they were alone, Christine wished she was Daddy's only child. She had fuzzy memories of the past being like that, but figured she was imagining things. Ma'am said Christine wasted too much time daydreaming and sometimes, she felt guilty for wanting Sam, Cass, Jamie and Josh out of the perfect picture inside her head.

Daddy had always encouraged her to read and used to put her on his lap while reading agricultural magazines. When she could read on her own, come rain or shine, Daddy took her to the library in Clarkesville on Saturday mornings.

He also taught them to speak properly, insisting that living in the country didn't mean they had to sound like Country Bumpkins.

As they passed a row of shops crammed against each other, Christine worked out how to bring up what was on her mind. When they got near to the one-story library building, she stopped, squinting up at Daddy and shading her eyes from the sun. "What would you do if I wasn't at home?"

He frowned. "What d'you mean?"

"I was wondering about your sister and how come we never visit her."

A little while passed before Daddy answered. "Celia and Ellie don't get along."

Christine thought about that for a moment. Two cars swished past, route taxis racing to pick up passengers. She shielded her face from the dust the vehicles whipped up and after the wind died down, asked another question. "D'you get along with your sister?"

"Yes. Sometimes, we talk when I go to the farm store in Hoopersville for supplies." He tipped his head sideways. "Chrissie, why are you asking these questions?"

She didn't answer right away, but continued walking. A few chains down the bumpy sidewalk, she stopped and tugged his hand. "Daddy, about your sister—"

"No more questions for now—"

Ignoring one of the lessons he'd drilled into her, Christine cut him off. "Daddy, why doesn't Ma'am love me?"

Although he avoided her gaze, Daddy wouldn't lie to her. She'd never asked anything like that before, so she gave him time to think things out before he answered.

"There is stuff you don't know, things you're too young to understand."

"Like what?" She cocked her eyebrow, knowing it made her look older than her eleven years. "She hates me. Why else would she treat me as if she's not my mother?"

Daddy's eyes went wide and then his brows formed a line. "Christine, stop this foolishness."

She pulled her hand away and slid it into her pocket. Daddy had never spoken to her so harshly.

He squeezed her shoulder and made her stop in the shade of a Naseberry tree. Bringing his face down to hers, he said, "Princess, I'm sorry, okay?"

She nodded, but a while passed before she felt like talking. "Did I say something wrong?"

"No, no, everything is fine."

They got moving again, but Christine struggled to keep up with him. Daddy stared at the ground and didn't say anything else, but kept an arm around her shoulder.

On the verandah of the library, Daddy wiped his forehead with the back of one hand, while holding his shirt away from his chest. The skin under Christine's arms was sticky, so she flapped both hands around to try and cool down.

Daddy wore his serious face, which meant she couldn't bug him anytime soon. Right now, the books were calling her name. She'd get on with that and ask the other questions on the way home. She'd just try not to upset him again.

"Come on, Daddy." She dragged him by the arm. "Let's go inside."

Christine walked up to the circular counter. "Good Morning, Miss King."

"Hello, Christine. Nice to see you again."

The librarian smiled, showing rows of perfect teeth.

"We're returning these," Daddy said, placing two books on the counter.

Christine went to a shelf nearby that was lined with girls' adventure stories. The library was heaven; a row of ceiling fans cooled the building, swishing to a quiet cha-cha-cha beat. She breathed in the smell of the wax polish rising from the concrete floor, and the musty odor coming from the rows of books. Staying there all day would be wonderful.

Still standing by the counter, Daddy took out a hanky and wiped his face. Christine couldn't figure out why he was acting so weird. She looked at him some more and then shrugged. Who ever knew what was going on with adults?

Miss King picked up the returned books, searched for the index cards in a narrow box and stuck them on the inside flap. Daddy stared at the counter until Miss King asked if he was okay. He blinked as if coming out of a daydream, and smiled. "I'm fine, thanks."

"You looked like you were a million miles away," Miss King said and clicked her teeth in a smile.

Daddy's eyes crinkled when Christine approached the counter with two books pressed to her chest. Miss King touched Daddy's arm. "You have one fine girl there, Mr. Simms. She'll go a long way. You take good care of her, you hear?"

"You can be sure of that," Daddy said, taking the books and laying them on the counter. Miss King removed the cards and stamped the return date on a leaf pasted inside the book.

"See you next week," she said, with a slight click from her dentures.

"Bye!" Christine waved and headed into the sunlight with Daddy, but her mind stayed on Miss King's teeth. When she first asked Daddy about them, he said Mrs. King had false teeth. Christine always had questions, which Daddy took time to answer without snapping. Ma'am was a whole different story.

Putting on her best smile, Christine asked, "Can we get an ice cream?"

Daddy laughed, touching her cheek. "Yup, as long as you don't tell."

This was their secret. Each week—even when he didn't have much money—Daddy bought an ice cream cone for her.

Though he never told her so, Christine knew she was Daddy's favourite. She saw it in his eyes, and at times they knew what the other was thinking without having to say anything. Sometimes he'd rub her cheek and call her his princess.

Christine figured she was the reason her parents quarreled all the time. In the last year, she realized that Ma'am saw Daddy's face when she looked at her. *'Yuh look just like yuh ugly Puppa!'* she'd say. Christine didn't mind because Ma'am only said it because she resembled Daddy most.

Tired of having Ma'am on her mind, Christine pushed her into the little room she reserved in her head and shut off the light. She concentrated on the Pistachio ice cream, delighting in the flavour. Home and what happened there, could stay until later.

They sat under an umbrella in front of Clarkesville's only pastry shop to enjoy their treat. Eyes closed, Christine licked the ice cream, letting it melt over her tongue. When she turned the cone for another swipe, she remembered the most important thing she wanted to ask Daddy.

"I still want to ask you something."

"What's that?"

She paused and took a deep breath. "D'you think you could live without me if you had to?"

Daddy's head cocked to one side. "We're back to that again? Why don't you just tell me what's on your mind?"

She stared at the grocery shop across the street. "Is your sister nice? What's she like?"

"Like me, I guess. She has one son, a little older than you, and she teaches primary school."

"When was the last time you saw her?"

"Last month." His eyebrows went up in a silent question. "Chrissie?"

Her words came in a rush. "I was wondering if I could go live with her."

Daddy's mouth opened and his forehead wrinkled.

Christine slumped on the edge of the table, knowing Daddy would say no.

He took her free hand. "Princess, you don't know my sister. The last time you saw her, you were eight. I can't ask her out of the blue to take one of my children. She'd believe I was losing my mind."

"But, Daddy—"

"Chrissie, I can't do that." Now he wouldn't look at her. "I know things are hard at home, but I'll do my best to make them better."

Heat swelled behind Christine's eyes and her chin trembled.

"Don't cry. Please." Daddy put his arm around her and kissed her forehead. "I just can't do it. What would I do without you, hmm?"

Pale green ice cream ran over her fingers and down her wrist. Daddy held the cone while wiping her hand with a napkin. Turning it over, he patted her eyes and mouth and when her tears wouldn't stop, he got out his hanky.

She hoped he'd change his mind. He didn't know half of what happened at home, and if she told him Ma'am would double her punishment.

Daddy gave her back the cone and cupped the side of her face. "I'll try," he said.

Christine gave him a wobbly smile and hugged him tight.

"You must be a witch or something," he muttered.

She grinned, feeling as if her birthday had come early. "What d'you mean?"

"You make it so hard to refuse anything you ask," he said, "but then, you never ask for much."

Christine closed her eyes and snuggled against Daddy, inhaling his scent, which reminded her of soap, sunshine and happy times. He hugged her again, and she had never loved him more than in that moment.

She crossed her fingers, praying for good luck. Auntie Rosita, her Sunday school teacher, had taught them about a humongous war in the Bible called Armageddon. As happy as she felt now, Christine couldn't help thinking that same war would come to their house when Ma'am heard her latest idea.

Chapter 4

Christine's mind strayed to Hoopersville, a place she had never seen. A book about a runaway teenager rested on her chest while she stared at the water stains on the ceiling.

She pictured a neat house with a small garden, a loving Aunt Celia and a firm bed, where she would sleep alone. In her mind, she came up with a fuzzy idea of what Aunt Celia looked like—a tall woman with a quiet voice, not like Ma'am, who shouted all the time. She couldn't remember if Aunt Celia had a husband, but she'd ask Daddy.

Would he take her to Hoopersville next week, if she asked? The only one who knew the town was Sam. Daddy said it was their special time, the boys' day out. He never took Sam to see Aunt Celia though, and Christine wondered about that. Why go to the farm store and not see his sister if she lived in the same town?

Josh's squeal cut through her thoughts. "Me now! Me now!"

Jamielle's laughter drowned his cries. Then Cass yelled, "No! It's my turn, Josh."

"Everybody will get a turn, okay?" Daddy's words stopped the bickering, and soon, laughter sliced through Christine's dream world again.

She rolled her eyes imagining Cass, Jamie and Josh pushing and crowding each other to get on Daddy's lap, or his back, for a 'jockey ride'.

Although Daddy had long days on the farm, every evening he spent at least an hour with the younger ones. He'd let them climb all over him while tickling them until they laughed so hard Ma'am told them to shut up. Though she was too old for that kind of game, Christine enjoyed watching her brother and sisters have fun. Today being Saturday, they would 'ride' Daddy until they were bored or tired.

At the next round of giggles, Christine bit her fingernail. If she could hear the noise, so could Ma'am.

As though Christine's thought had made it happen, Ma'am yelled. "You ca'an play without all this noise?"

"They're just enjoying themselves, Ellie."

She pictured Daddy waving at Ma'am and telling her to relax. If Christine timed it right, Ma'am would dart back to her bedroom and slam the door loud enough to rattle the entire house.

Christine held her breath and tilted her head. The blast came seconds later and in the silence that followed, her sisters whispered and giggled.

If things worked out as she hoped, Christine would soon be out of the house. She'd miss her siblings and most of all, Daddy. She wouldn't miss Ma'am for a second. Only Josh got any love from her. Most of the time she ignored Sam, Cassandra and Jamielle.

Even before the others came along, Christine couldn't remember spending time with Ma'am and doing the things normal parents did with their children. Christine used to occupy herself playing in the yard, but those days passed quickly as the family got bigger. Seven people took a lot of caring for, and Christine learned to do it well as she grew older.

When Ma'am wasn't chasing Josh, she was screaming at Christine, who tried to keep Cass and Jamie out of Ma'am's way. Sam was smart. He learned to stay out of the house in the summer months, doing whatever boys did outside all day.

On school days, he spent the afternoons in the room he shared with Josh, but Christine was not so lucky. She had to keep the house in order and babysit.

Christine had known for a while that something was wrong with Ma'am. When she wasn't angry, she stared into space, smiling at nothing. Sometimes she asked the same questions again and again, rubbed her forehead, and frowned for no reason.

No matter how hard she thought about it, Christine didn't know anybody else who acted like Ma'am, and was sure her smoking didn't help her sickness. She was much calmer when she smoked the awful-smelling cigarettes, but her good mood didn't last long.

When Christine first asked Daddy if Ma'am was sick in her head, he didn't give a straight answer. He said she would get better, but Christine knew about the bottle of pills in the bathroom cupboard that Ma'am used for her headaches. She said they made her jumpy so she stopped taking them, although Daddy insisted that she stay on them.

During one argument, Ma'am tore up the prescription and scattered the pieces on the living room floor. Afterward, she told Daddy she wasn't going back to the doctor and as far as Christine knew, she didn't.

A weight landed on Christine, squeezing her chest. "Ow! Careful!"

Cassandra and Jamielle flopped across her body in a giggling heap of elbows and knees. Christine pulled the book from under the crush of bodies and shoved it beneath a pillow. She made a scary face, growled and tickled Cass and Jamie. They squealed, scrabbled out of the bed and thundered down the hallway. Behind them, Christine moved toward the kitchen on light feet.

Ma'am yelled from her room. "How many times mus' I tell you kids not to run through the house?"

The girls scampered through the kitchen and out the door. Christine followed them, but stopped on the back verandah where Daddy sat in one of the patio chairs with his ankles crossed on the low wall. The lines on his forehead told Christine he was thinking hard.

When Daddy saw her, he smiled and patted the seat. Cass ran across the grass to the steps, barefooted and sweaty. She'd have to bathe again before dinner, Christine thought.

"Chris, you're not coming? We playing hide-and-seek," Cass said.

Daddy corrected her. "*We're* playing."

Cass repeated his words, hopping from one foot to the other.

"Naw, I'm staying here with Daddy," Christine said, shaking her head.

"Okay." Cass jumped backward off the step. The two puppies ran after her, leaving their mother resting in the shade of the Mango tree.

"Enjoying your book?" Daddy asked.

Christine dragged her gaze from the sleeping dog and nodded. They sat in silence for a while before Christine touched his arm and glanced at the open doorway. "You know Ma'am is getting worse, right?"

He sighed, but didn't answer.

"She needs a doctor. She's yelling all the time and…" Christine grabbed his arm. *"You should make her go."*

His chest lifted and warm air drifted over her when he breathed out. "I know. I'll deal with it soon."

His arm eased around her, and Christine got the same sense of peace as when she looked at the mountains through the bedroom window. Even when Daddy wasn't at home, she felt better knowing he'd be back at the end of the day. Their earlier conversation flashed through her mind. She looked up at him, suddenly anxious. "You won't forget what we talked about today, will you?"

"No, I won't."

She closed her eyes, hoping he'd get a chance to talk to Aunt Celia soon.

"Maxwell." Ma'am stood in the doorway, arms akimbo. "I want to talk to you."

Though she wanted to draw closer to Daddy, Christine thought it best to leave. She sprang off the chair, avoiding Ma'am's wild eyes.

"Maxwell, come inside. Christine, stay."

Christine sank on the seat, eyes fixed on her toes while Daddy followed Ma'am into the house.

Her words floated to Christine. "What you two whispering about?"

Christine didn't hear Daddy's reply because a door slammed. She slumped, relieved that Ma'am hadn't wanted to blame her for anything or order her to do any chores.

The yard turned grey under a cloud cover, which lasted a few minutes. The sun tried to come back out, but had lost its warmth as the heat of the day gave way to evening.

Christine told herself to relax. Nothing was wrong if Ma'am wanted to speak with Daddy in private. They did it all the time. She closed her eyes and breathed out, surprised at the chilliness of the sudden breeze that rolled over her skin and swept a bunch of leaves across the yard.

Ma'am shouted, and Christine's eyes snapped open. Her words made no sense and from the screechiness of her voice, Ma'am was at the beginning of a bad fit.

Glass broke. Daddy bellowed, his words unclear.

Christine drew her legs up, circling them with her arms. She hid her face, praying this argument had nothing to do with her wish to live with Aunt Celia.

She rocked herself. Faster and faster she went, eyes closed, sweat running off her forehead. *Please God, let Daddy win this argument.*

A bang shook the house. Ma'am's screeching grated across Christine's skin.

Daddy shouted. "Ellie, be reasonable—"

"The answer is no! If you think I'm going to let you—"

Something made of glass shattered, which meant Ma'am was throwing things again.

Christine raised her head, gulping air as if someone was stealing it from her lungs as fast as she could take it in. Her face and arms were sticky with sweat. She wiped both eyes on her sleeves to stop the tears, while wishing the fighting would end. Somebody was bound to get hurt one day.

Cass and Jamie skipped up the steps and plopped down on the seat beside Christine, smelling of sweat. Daddy and Ma'am's voices came again, even louder. Both girls looked at each other, their smiles disappeared, and Jamie's thumb went into her mouth. She leaned against Christine and Cass huddled next to Jamie, clasping her hand.

Christine wiped her eyes again, smiling to reassure her sisters that everything would be fine, despite the rise and fall of their parents' angry voices.

A moment of silence wrapped around them. Even the wind stopped teasing the leaves on the Mango tree. The only noise came from Jamie, who continued sucking her finger. Usually, it annoyed Christine. Now, it didn't bother her.

Ma'am yelled, "Let me go, you piece of filth!"

Her words were loud enough for people to hear over the mountain and in whatever village lay beyond. Her sisters didn't need to hear any curse words, so Christine pointed to the puppies nipping at each other by the shed. "Go play with Tim and Trixie."

Cass and Jamie edged off the seat and walked into the fading sunlight, looking back at Christine.

Pounding footsteps came from the kitchen, sending a jolt up Christine's back. She turned to peek between the window blades. Through the sheer curtain, she watched Ma'am, who stood in front of the counter pulling the drawers open and slamming them shut. She muttered, not even pausing for breath, while the cutlery rattled. For a few seconds, she squeezed her head between both hands.

Christine sat still, hoping Ma'am wouldn't think to call her to find whatever she needed.

Ma'am pulled open the drawer nearest the wall and rooted inside. The clanging of metal echoed around the kitchen. She straightened up and Christine shook when she saw what Ma'am held in her hand. Ma'am ran out of the kitchen, clutching the knife and shouting. "Maxwell, I swear to God…"

The world went a dizzying white. Christine sped into the house, running down the passage, forgetting what would happen to her for committing that particular crime.

To stop herself from flying past her parents' bedroom, Christine hung on to the door frame. Daddy and Ma'am shouted together, reminding Christine of a dog fight. She wanted to cover her ears, but couldn't. Not when things were this bad.

Combs, brushes and bottles clattered to the floor, as Ma'am threw them at Daddy. Then she grabbed something shiny from the bed and flung herself at him. Daddy held on to Ma'am, one arm stretched across her back, as if they were hugging. With his other hand, Daddy grabbed Ma'am's wrist. The knife in her hand had a long, narrow blade, which made Christine shudder.

To Christine, they seemed locked in a wild dance, rocking side to side. They stumbled and then steadied themselves against each other. Ma'am pushed hard, trying to get free.

Christine whispered while they struggled. "No…no…no!"

Her head swung back and forth and her body trembled like a leaf whipped by a strong wind. She wanted to do something, but her feet didn't obey when she told them to move.

Ma'am twisted and flopped around like she had gone mad. Daddy held on tight, still trying to get hold of the knife. A flash of yellow on the floor caught Christine's eyes. She whimpered and rushed to Daddy, desperate to stop him from getting hurt.

Daddy stepped on Josh's plastic car, staggered and let go of Ma'am. She jumped at him and her hand came down twice. At first, there was no blood. Then a red line appeared on Daddy's tee-shirt and blood gushed out of his neck.

Christine backed away trying to find something to hold on to, but it was like searching in the dark. Her world stopped and she stood still, while her eyes tried to tear their way out of her head. She clamped her hands to the sides of her face.

This had to be a bad dream.

Ma'am stood watching daddy, her mouth hanging open and her eyes bulging as if she couldn't believe what she was seeing.

Daddy looked at his chest and then met Christine's eyes. He lurched to where she stood and crashed to his knees, using one hand to hold himself upright. He pressed the other hand to his chest, his shoulders moving rapidly as he tried to breathe. Blood pumped from the wound in his neck, turning his white tee-shirt dark red.

Christine shook her head, unfreezing her brain. She dropped in front of him, screaming. "Daddy!"

His lips moved, but only a gurgle and pink spit came out. Christine pushed against Daddy's shoulders, trying to see his face. She lifted his head, shouting into his face, now the colour of ashes. "Daddy!"

His eyes were half-open, his breathing shallow. His lips moved again. Christine pressed her ear against them. His breath barely tickled her skin.

"What? What?" she asked, as if she were the parent and he, the child.

"Christine, I'm...so...sorry." He gurgled, still trying to talk while blood dribbled from his mouth.

With one hand, Christine wiped away the blood. Daddy's eyelids fluttered and then closed. Another scream built in Christine's throat, but Daddy squeezed the breath out of her as he toppled forward, crushing her. She pushed him away and let out a cry when he crumpled to the floor on his side, halfway into the passage.

She sank back staring, her fingers covering her mouth, her brain sending the same message, again and again.

Do something!

She laid a hand on Daddy's chest, searching for the regular thumping of his heart. She felt nothing. Blood sprang between her fingers and continued to ooze as if being called to join the spreading circle that seeped into the floorboards. The rusty taste of blood flowed over her tongue, forcing her to swallow.

Ma'am came to the doorway, still gripping the knife. She looked down at them, her eyes blank as if nothing out of the ordinary had happened. She moved away, sitting when the back of her knees touched the bed.

The knife fell and spun under the bed.

Ma'am's silence and the huge whites of her eyes made Christine want to run out of the room, but she couldn't leave Daddy, nor could she take her eyes off Ma'am. No telling what she'd do next.

Ma'am's face twisted, she squeezed her forehead, and let out a shriek that sent Christine scrabbling away. Sobbing and shouting words Christine didn't understand, Ma'am threw herself across the bed.

A door opened, and Josh shot into the passage. He ran to her, hands held out. "Kwistee."

Sam grabbed at him, but not before Josh's feet went out from under him as he slid into Daddy's blood. Josh tried to get up, but skidded around, howling when he couldn't stand.

Grabbing Josh by his tee-shirt, Sam lifted him out of the mess. When he stepped away, Sam's mouth moved without a sound coming out. His eyes looked ready to escape their sockets. Leaning against the wall, he slid down and sat. Sam didn't do anything about the blood from Josh's legs and clothes that stained his shirt, nor did he look away from Daddy's body.

The unfamiliar odor and taste of Daddy's blood churned Christine's stomach. Josh continued to cry, stretching his arms to Christine. When Sam wouldn't let him go, Josh struggled, screaming louder.

Cass and Jamie ran from the kitchen into the passage. "What's happening?"

Christine stood on feet that didn't seem to know how to work anymore and tried to turn her sisters toward the kitchen. They refused to move and peeked on either side of her with wide eyes.

Living around animals meant they had seen death before, but none of them had ever experienced it like this. Nor had they ever seen so much blood. Cass and Jamie hung on to Christine and sobbed into her shirt.

Christine didn't stop to think, but put one foot in front of the other, taking Cass and Jamie with her. She seated them at the kitchen table, mixed two glasses of syrupy sugar and water and told them to drink. Ma'am used to do that whenever one of them hit their head while playing, so maybe it would help them calm down.

Christine faced the passage, staring into Daddy's face, conscious of her tears when her vision went blurry. She dragged the back of her hands across her eyes, but they filled again. She realized then that Sam hadn't moved from where he'd been sitting. Josh continued wailing, and Sam did nothing to make him stop.

A sense of responsibility dragged her back to Daddy's body. She didn't look at him or think about what his stillness meant.

She called Sam's name, but he didn't answer. Instead, he glared at Ma'am who lay on the bed with her shoulders heaving.

"Sam!" This time Christine shook him.

He turned his head and looked at her, his cheeks covered by red smudges.

Christine avoided looking at his messy shirt, staring at the wall behind him. "Go to the kitchen. Keep an eye on Cass and Jamie. I'm going to get help."

Was she doing the right thing, leaving them in the house with Ma'am? What if she went mad and killed them all?

Christine shook off her doubts. Ma'am had already done the worst she could do. Christine was the only other person she would hurt.

As Sam pushed away from the wall to follow her instructions, Josh stopped wailing. Christine glanced into her parents' room. Her mother lay curled up on the bed, talking to herself and then giggling.

Christine heart pumped as if she had been running. A strange sensation that didn't yet have a name settled inside her, filling her chest.

She cut her eyes at the woman who was supposed to love and care for her, feeling the years of abuse churning, coiling and settling into something solid.

That thing was hate.

Her mother had taken away the one thing that made life bearable—her relationship with Daddy.

Christine's eyes filled again while she put on her slippers. That done, she shuffled down the steps into the yard.

She walked without seeing anything. Nor did she hurry. What was most important was in the past. Gone. Swept away like the leaves that spun and disappeared in the gutter when they had heavy rainfall.

For the moment, she felt nothing, as though she had been turned upside down and everything inside her shaken out. Earlier in the day, she fancied the house mats must have felt lighter when she hung them over the line and beat the dirt from them until not a single puff of dust remained.

She didn't feel lighter; she was empty. She didn't think about where she was going. Her feet knew the way to get there.

Things were the same as they had always been.

The sun was on its way below the horizon. The last of the evening breeze rustled in the trees. The cows chewed their cud in the pastures that stretched along both sides of the road.

Yet everything had changed.

The steady trickle of tears surged into a flood and Christine sobbed as if her heart was breaking.

Chapter 5

C hristine followed the road for a quarter of a mile until she came to the rutted track that led to the neighboring farm. The Powell's were friends of the family and had a telephone. They could call for help, not that it would do any good.

Christine stopped by the side of the road and closed her eyes, hoping she had imagined everything. But when she looked down, her dress and hands were still bloody. Gulping back another crop of sobs and struggling to see through her tears, Christine trudged toward the Powell's home.

The dogs met her with excited barks while she opened the wood-and-barbed-wire gate, shut it behind her and then walked toward the house sitting at the crest of the hill. The three mongrels crowded her ankles, wanting their chins scratched. It was a ritual, but Christine couldn't stop to play. She waved them away, but they ran up the hill panting and keeping close to her side.

As she dragged her feet closer to the house, Mrs. Powell—Aunt Icy to her family—walked onto the verandah. Aunt Icy and her husband was the closest Christine came to having grandparents.

She stood akimbo, head cocked to one side. When she recognized Christine, Aunt Icy smiled and her eyes sank into a crisscross of wrinkles. She wiped both hands on her apron and then held them out to Christine. "How you do?"

While she scanned Christine's clothes, her smile dimmed and then disappeared. "Christine, is what happen?"

Christine stumbled up the steps and flung herself into Aunt Icy's arms. She sobbed while Aunt Icy rubbed her back and made comforting sounds. "You not goin' to tell me wha' happen to you, child?"

Aunt Icy's heart raced against Christine's ear, but she couldn't answer. When she raised her head, Aunt Icy fumbled with the pocket of her apron and pressed a wad of tissue into Christine's hand. She took it, dried her eyes and blew her nose. Aunt Icy pulled her over to a chair and made her sit.

After shooting several glances between Christine's face and dress, Aunt Icy made a weird sound in her throat and spoke louder. "What happen' at home, child? You have to tell me this minute."

Her question brought on a fresh bout of crying. After a few minutes, Christine rolled her eyes toward the ceiling and squeezed them shut. She stopped her hands from trembling by wrapping them around her body.

"Ma'am used a knife on Daddy. I think he's dead. His heart wasn't beating."

Aunt Icy put a hand to her neck. She swallowed so hard her head bobbed. "Where yuh brothers and sisters?"

"At home. I told Sam to watch them."

Aunt Icy rubbed her forehead. "Where yuh mother?"

Christine insides heaved with anger and she spat words between them. "In bed."

"In bed?" Aunt Icy squinted at her before turning toward the doorway. "I soon come. I goin' to make a call."

She moaned and shuffled away on arthritic knees. Ever since Christine had known Aunt Icy, she'd complained that arthritis made her life miserable.

Christine stared at the crabgrass covering the yard, seeing nothing but green fuzz. Praying hard, she pressed both hands together. What if she had dreamed Daddy was dead? Maybe she wasn't yet awake, but was in bed in the middle of a nightmare. That would explain everything, but she had never felt this bad in a dream.

Aunt Icy came back and moved to the railing, where she cupped her hands around her mouth and hollered. "Vernon!"

Seconds later, a voice responded. "Oy?"

Aunt Icy made a trumpet of her hands again. "Come now!"

Her husband answered. "Oy."

He came hobbling up the track and entered the yard as fast as his bowed legs allowed. Leaning forward, he climbed the slope, grunting with the effort of moving more quickly than his usual speed.

When he stood on the verandah, he pulled a bandana out of his pocket. After removing his straw hat, Uncle Vernon dabbed his face and wiped his bald head. Sweat stained the front of his khaki work shirt in a deep upside down triangle.

"Christine." He acknowledged her with a wave, and a twitch of his beard. He tore his gaze away from her dress before turning to face Aunt Icy. "Is what happen?"

Aunt Icy flapped her apron, glanced at Christine and spoke in a low voice. "Ellie stab Maxwell. Sound like him might be dead. I called the police."

"Jesus. I goin' get the Jeep." He hurried away, rocking side to side on his bandy legs.

Aunt Icy slipped inside and came back with a wet cloth, which she used to clean Christine's face and hands. The rag soothed from a distance, as if a cloud of cotton candy had wrapped itself around her. Christine wished she could stay there all day.

Christine sat in the back of the Land Rover, gazing at the shadows outside the window. If today was an ordinary day, she would have been ecstatic, because she could count the number of times she had ridden in a vehicle.

Everything in Sheaville was in walking distance, so they only drove anywhere once in a while. But what did that matter now?

Closing her eyes, she pushed away the thoughts that tried to crowd her mind. She was good at blocking out the things she didn't want to remember. She had two favourite daydreams; one was of a different life with just Daddy and her and the other was imagining the other side of the John Crow Mountains. Now one dream was dead. She sighed, forcing herself to picture a house and a family that lived beyond the mountains. Why couldn't she have been born over there?

The sound of her name jolted Christine back into the vehicle. Aunt Icy stood outside holding the door open.

Christine was home.

Her tummy hurt at the thought of going into the house. Daddy was inside, just as she had left him. Unless by some miracle he had recovered, but this was her life and things like that never happened.

Though she felt as if she'd fall, Christine slid out of the Land Rover, forcing her feet to work. The puppies raced over and rubbed against her ankles, but she nudged them away and climbed the steps. At the top, she spun back and stumbled down, motioning to Aunt Icy and Uncle Vernon to go around to the back of the house. She couldn't go past Daddy.

The kitchen door was still open and everybody, except Josh, sat where she had left them. Sam's head rested on his folded hands. Cass sniffled and picked at a scab on her knee. Jamie sucked her thumb and played with one of her plaits. Josh went around the table making vrooming noises, a plastic airplane clutched in his hand.

Christine looked away from the dried blood on his skin and clothing.

Aunt Icy examined all the children before holding on to Josh's arm to stop him. With a gentle hand, she shook Sam's shoulder.

He raised his head, facing them with red, swollen eyes.

"Where's your mother?" Aunt Icy asked.

Sam pointed down the passage. "In the bedroom."

Christine took Josh's hand to allow Aunt Icy to follow her husband farther into the house. The smell of blood filled her nose, and she didn't want to go near Daddy again, but she lifted Josh onto a chair and then followed the couple, switching on the passage light. Uncle Vernon called as he went down the corridor. "Ellie?"

He stopped at the second doorway and looked in. His wife peeked around him and nudged him aside, skirting the body as she went into the room. The light switch clicked on while Uncle Vernon bent over Daddy.

"Ellie?" Aunt Icy called.

Christine didn't hear an answer. Aunt Icy left the room to stand behind Uncle Vernon, who picked up Daddy's hand and pressed his wrist. Gently, Uncle Vernon laid Daddy's hand back on the floor. He looked up at Aunt Icy and shook his head. He groaned, held on to his knees and stood up straight. Turning to Christine, he put an arm around her shoulders and took her to the kitchen. He sat her in a chair and left again.

Aunt Icy and Uncle Vernon disappeared into her parents' room and their voices came to her as a low hum. She hoped they were deciding what to do about her mother. Time stopped and then an age passed before Uncle Vernon spread a sheet over Daddy.

The two adults came into the kitchen, looking at the floor and blinking hard. The air around the dining table hung heavy. Even Josh was quiet where he sat in Christine's lap, the airplane still clasped in his fist. He laid his head on Christine's chest, and her arms folded around him.

A white police car arrived with nothing more than a half note from the siren. The only time things got exciting in Sheaville was when the fire truck was on its way to a burning building and that didn't happen often.

Christine guessed the police didn't want to frighten them by arriving with the siren going at full blast. She squeezed Josh to her chest, pushing away her anxiety over what would happen to them. Aunt Icy patted her shoulder, as if she knew what Christine was thinking.

Uncle Vernon went out to meet the officers and waved them toward him. Two men clomped into the kitchen behind Uncle Vernon, who introduced them as Detective Baines and Constable Brown. Detective Baines was thin, and resembled a long sliver of Guinea grass, while Constable Brown looked like he'd swallowed a barrel.

Uncle Vernon leaned his head toward the passage and the policemen looked at where Daddy's body lay.

Christine knew both men from passing the police station everyday on her way to and from school. Never had she imagined the police might have a reason to come to her house.

One of the officers coughed and cleared his throat. "Did anybody touch anything?"

Uncle Vernon shrugged and looked at Christine. She said nothing, but pressed her lips together. How was she supposed to remember, when her whole world was smashed to bits?

"Where is Mrs. Simms?" asked Constable Brown.

"In the bedroom," Uncle Vernon answered.

"Doing what?" the detective asked, frowning.

Both adults replied. "Sleeping."

The detective tipped his head toward the adults. "You said sleeping?"

Uncle Vernon and Aunt Icy nodded while the police officers exchanged frowns.

Christine stared after them until they stood over her father, and the sheet that had turned burgundy around the edges. One officer bent over, lifted the cloth and felt Daddy's wrist, as Uncle Vernon had done. The other took careful steps into the bedroom.

"Mrs. Simms, Mrs. Simms!" he called.

Before Christine could look away, the Constable walked out of the bedroom holding on to Ma'am's arm. Christine trembled and pressed her back to the chair.

By that time, the Detective stood outside, speaking on a cellular phone. He'd warned them as he went past. "Nobody touch anything."

"Where you taking me?" Ma'am asked.

"To the station," said the Constable.

"Station? I ca'an leave the chil'ren!"

Weird expressions chased over Ma'am's face while her eyeballs danced and she struggled to loose the policeman's grip on her arm. Her plaits stuck out in several directions, and she screwed up her mouth as though vexed. Christine avoided staring at the splotches of blood on her floral blouse.

When Ma'am spotted Christine, she tried twisting out of the policeman's grip. "Is her fault! Is all her fault! Is she cause me to kill Maxwell!"

She struggled to escape, straining toward Christine. "I goin' get rid o' you too!"

The Constable carried Ma'am toward the door, while she screamed and bit at him. The shrieks echoed inside Christine's head. Josh climbed from her lap, attempting to follow their mother, but Sam held him back. Josh screeched, trying to pry Sam's fingers off his wrist.

Christine sprang up, knocking over her chair. She turned toward the passage, but couldn't move. She'd have to pass Daddy. She also couldn't go outside because it was dark, and Ma'am continued yelling a string of bad words. Aunt Icy opened her arms and Christine flung herself into them. "It's not my fault! It's not my fault!"

"I know child, I know."

The sobs hitched in Christine's chest and she cried harder when Aunt Icy whispered, "Never mind, mi dear."

When her tears slowed, Christine reminded herself that her siblings took their lead from her. She'd always tried to make them feel secure no matter what was going on in their home, but a moment ago, she would have burst if she didn't get to cry away some of her guilt. Right now, she had to be strong.

She stepped away from Aunt Icy, dragging her hands across her face. Uncle Vernon handed Aunt Icy a handkerchief, which she crushed to her eyes.

In the yard, a spot of light moved to and fro. Christine flipped the switch by the door, flooding the back verandah and the yard with light. The detective glanced toward the house and continued smoking a cigarette, blowing rings into the air.

Though Ma'am still screamed curse words, Christine couldn't see her because the police had parked the car out front.

The cigarette smoke made Christine's nose itch and she looked at the officer again. Why couldn't she be one of his children? Then she wouldn't be here, trying to get through something she could never have imagined.

She closed her eyes to hide from her siblings' tears. Sam, Cass and Jamie had joined Josh, weeping quietly. Uncle Vernon put an arm around Aunt Icy and nudged her toward the verandah.

Christine sat, patting Cass' arm while she watched the two adults through the curtain. Uncle Vernon hugged Aunt Icy, while she cried and muttered into his neck. Christine frowned and concentrated on her words.

"...thing Maxwell feared most in life, overtake him children in death, Vernon."

"Ah, Icy..."

She blew her nose and stood with her back to the window. "What goin' happen to those poor children?"

Christine waited for his answer, but he shrugged and looked down. Then, he covered his face with one hand. She assumed he was thinking, until his shoulders lifted and fell several times. His body shimmered before her, and Christine turned her head away as Uncle Vernon wept.

Chapter 6

Christine didn't want to spend the night in the house where Daddy was murdered. She stopped worrying about it after Aunt Icy said they were going to stay at her house.

The police had questioned the older children before giving the Powell's permission to keep them overnight at their farm since there was nowhere else for them to go.

By that time, another police car arrived, as well as a van with McLaren's Funeral Services printed on the side.

The police photographed everything, including them. Then they changed their clothes and the police took the bloodstained items they had worn.

Aunt Icy helped Christine pack a few things, which took a while. Christine tried not to look at their clothing, which was clean, but worn thin.

Shopping was another thing Ma'am rarely bothered to do for them, which meant all their clothes were too short or tight.

Aunt Icy's brows wrinkled as she went through each drawer, putting items aside and choosing others. Finally, they were ready to go. On their way out, they left the police still moving around her parents' bedroom and the passage.

They drove to the farm, squished together in the back of the Jeep. Christine was too numb to care about Jamielle's elbow jammed into her side, and nobody else complained about being squeezed.

After washing up and eating, Christine welcomed Aunt Icy's instructions for them to turn in for the night. In bed, Christine swished her legs on top of the crisp, cotton sheets. At home, theirs was knotty from the poor quality of the material and overuse. Nothing got replaced at their house until they fell apart, because Ma'am's sickness made her too tired to do anything.

Christine yawned, eyes burning from exhaustion and too much crying. Her sisters had already fallen asleep. She turned on her side, snuggled against Jamielle and told herself she couldn't do anything about their situation, so she might as well get some sleep.

Christine opened her eyes, but didn't recognize the ceiling, the room or know which day of the week it was. She thought for a few seconds.

Sunday. It was Sunday and Daddy was dead.

The memory of Daddy on the floor surrounded by blood came back, hurting a thousand times worse than one of Ma'am's slaps. Christine shook her head to get rid of that picture and gazed out the window where grey clouds hung low in the sky. How well the weather matched her mood.

She hoped Ma'am was still at the police station and that she'd stay there forever. Taking a deep breath, Christine recalled the conversation when Daddy agreed to ask his sister to let her live with her.

Maybe if she hadn't asked to leave home he'd still be alive. Daddy's wish for her to be happy had probably started this last argument. Tears burned her eyes, ran down the sides of her face and into her hair. Daddy was dead because of her. Ma'am was right. It *was* her fault. Christine turned on her belly and sobbed into the pillow.

When she stopped crying, Christine woke her brothers and sisters and helped the younger ones dress themselves. After they washed their faces and brushed their teeth, she led them to the Powell's living room.

Aunt Icy greeted them and took them into the dining room, where she served liver and boiled, green bananas. Christine had no appetite and used her fork to push the bananas around the plate. Sam and Cass ate as if they hadn't eaten in a week, while Jamie and Josh played with their food.

"Christine, why yuh not eating?" Aunt Icy asked.

"I'm not hungry."

"Yuh have to eat something to keep up yuh energy." Aunt Icy pulled out a chair and sat beside Christine. "I talk to yuh auntie last night—"

"You know my auntie?" Christine looked up, surprised.

"Yes, she grow up same place in yuh house." Aunt Icy tapped Christine under the chin. "She coming here today and will have to make arrangements for Maxwell's..."

She paused, and Christine stirred in the seat. "Aunt Icy, what's going to happen to us? What will the police do with my mother?"

"Child, I don' know. Yuh have to ask yuh auntie."

Aunt Icy got to her feet, patting Christine's shoulder. "I'm sure everything goin' to work out all right. Celia will know what to do."

With her chin propped in her hand, Christine eyed the colourful Plaster of Paris plaques on the wall, including one that said *God Bless This Home*. They had to be older than her, because Christine had never seen them anywhere else. They made the room cozy.

How she longed for a comfortable place like this, where nobody shouted, but they couldn't stay long. Christine knew that much. She played with a bit of fried liver, wondering what her aunt would say when she came.

Sam, Cass, Jamielle and Josh continued to eat and didn't seem worried. She couldn't blame them. Compared to what they ate at home, this breakfast was a feast.

She wished the lump in her stomach would move, but knew it wouldn't until she found a way around their problem. Aunt Celia probably couldn't keep them, so Christine didn't let her mind go there.

If she could have one wish, it would be that she was someone else. A girl with loving parents and no worries, but her life was way different.

Her reality was that she'd always taken care for her brothers and sisters, so it was nobody else's responsibility but hers to make certain they stayed together.

Chapter 7

C lose your mouth, Christine told herself while pressing her face to the curtain.

Celia Jennings resembled Daddy so much it made Christine gasp and suck the sheer drape to her lips by accident. Pushing the material aside, Christine studied her aunt.

She had Daddy's squarish face and kind eyes. The hair above her ears was turning grey and she was the tallest woman Christine had ever seen.

Aunt Celia hugged Aunt Icy the minute she got out of her little red car. While Aunt Icy spoke, Aunt Celia frowned.

She had lines in her forehead like Daddy. She had more, but that was okay since she was ten years older, according to Daddy.

Christine guessed Aunt Icy was telling their aunt everything she didn't say when they spoke on the phone last night. Christine moved from the window to the sofa and sat with the others, biting down on her impatience. When they came into the living room, Aunt Icy told Aunt Celia to sit.

Her shoes were shiny and her handbag looked as though it was made of leather. The suit she wore was as good, maybe better than those in the shop windows in town. Christine was so absorbed with her aunt's clothing, she didn't respond when she spoke the first time.

"Christine?" Her aunt leaned forward to get her attention.

Christine jerked and stood up as if someone had poked her with a pin. "Yes!"

"Sit, sit." Aunt Celia waved her back into the seat, smiling.

Christine, Sam, Cass, Jamielle and Josh sat in a line on the largest of the sofas. A glance at them told Christine they were also fascinated by the similarities between Daddy and their aunt.

She had to be wondering why they were staring at her like that, but it was as if she was wearing Daddy's face.

"I'm Celia. Your father's sister," she said, looking at them one at a time.

Aunt Celia's mouth drooped and she looked as sad as Christine felt. She forced a smile, then spoke to Christine. "D'you remember me?"

"A little."

Christine looked down when Cass slipped a hand into hers. She squeezed it just as Aunt Celia started talking again.

"I remember all of you from my visit a few years ago. Well everybody except Josh, who wasn't born yet. Perhaps I should tell you something about myself and then I'll ask each of you to tell me a little about yourselves. Is that okay?"

The children nodded, and while they spoke, Christine stared at the printed lace hugging the arms and back of the couch. They were much brighter than the ones at their house.

Christine's thoughts strayed to Daddy as she last saw him. With a tiny shake of the head, she replaced that scene with another—Daddy smiling and teasing her, tugging one of her plaits.

When Aunt Celia finished talking to them, she asked Christine to walk with her to the car. In the shade of a Plum tree, she took Christine's hand. "I wanted to speak to you in private. Maxwell kept me up to date on your progress, so I feel I know everybody." She drew a deep breath and continued, "In the absence of your mother and father, I'm your guardian. You understand?"

Christine nodded, but said nothing.

"It's unlikely that your mother will be released any time soon. I'll have to make permanent arrangements for all of you. You'll be staying here, with Aunt Icy, at least until the end of the week."

The wind fluttered the leaves above them, letting the sun through to create shifting patterns on their skin and the ground. Christine made circles in the grass with her bare toes, watching the moving shadows.

"I'll be making funeral arrangements for your father," Aunt Celia said, clearing her throat.

Christine looked up then. Aunt Celia's voice was uneven when she spoke again. "I'm off to the funeral home now, but I'll be back later."

Christine's eyes filled and she dipped her head.

Aunt Celia sighed and squeezed Christine's hand. "I know this is hard for you. It's difficult for me too. Although I didn't see Maxwell as often as I should have, I loved him."

She let go of Christine, faced the grassy field beyond the fence and went silent. When she spoke again, Christine got the feeling Aunt Celia had forgotten her. "Now, I'm responsible for five children, plus my own."

Sniffing, she gripped Christine's shoulder. "I can't tell you everything will be okay, but I'll do the best I can for all of you."

After Aunt Celia got inside the Suzuki and wiped the corners of her eyes, she drove out of the yard.

Dragging her feet, Christine climbed the steps and went into the house. Aunt Celia's words didn't make her feel any better and now worry filled her stomach, rolling and twisting as though it was alive.

What would she tell her brothers and sisters, seeing that she had no new information and where would they go?

Chapter 8

Christine didn't know how she'd survive Daddy's funeral. The thought of not ever seeing him again was unbearable, so she avoided dwelling on it.

Her body was an empty coconut husk, for she had cried herself dry. She did everything for her brothers and sisters, without thinking.

She fixed Cassandra's hair, detached from her cries as the comb went through her thick curls. Jamielle got away with jumping on Christine's chest without being scolded about her sharp elbows, and Christine bathed Josh, without caring that her clothes got soaked each time he splashed and giggled in the tub.

The autopsy was done within two weeks and the funeral took place on Wednesday afternoon. Since it was summer, they didn't need to get letters of excuse for absence from school. Christine wondered how she'd fill the two months that stretched ahead. Summer school was no longer a certainty.

Aunt Celia arranged the service at the Anglican Church the family attended. The building was several hundred years old, its walls made of brick, and the wooden benches worn smooth from regular use. The stained-glass windows contained biblical scenes, which kept Christine's mind occupied during Sunday sermons.

Mournful music blaring from the hearse made Christine's eyes water. During the ride she tried to forget that Daddy's body lay in a casket behind them, waiting to be put into the ground at the end of the service.

To Christine's relief, Ma'am did not get permission to attend the funeral.

The attendants, who reminded Christine of two sober blackbirds, placed the casket at the entrance of the church. Those who wished to do so, viewed Maxwell Simms' body.

Christine stood over Daddy, unwilling to believe this was the last time she'd see him. Aunt Icy had taken the others away after they looked at him. Jamie cried at the sight of Daddy lying motionless inside the coffin and Josh had called to him, wriggling his fingers for Daddy to take him from Aunt Icy.

Daddy almost looked the way he did when he slept on the sofa, but his face wasn't the same. He was darker and smoother from the stuff the funeral home put on his skin.

Christine prodded his folded hands and then pressed down on them. Their slight chill made her shudder and she thought maybe he'd wake up if he knew she needed him. Her touch didn't rouse him and she accepted the fact that he was gone. She studied his face to be sure she'd never forget him.

Aunt Celia came to her side and led her away from the coffin to allow the attendants to close and wheel it down the aisle for the start of the service.

The white casket had a mountain of pale lilies on top. Aunt Celia had said the service would be short, which was good because the church was warm from all the bodies stuffed inside.

Every family in Sheaville had come to pay their respect. Christine recognized people from nearby Clarkesville and was grateful Aunt Celia had gone shopping for them.

Christine ran her fingers over the see-through chiffon covering her black, linen dress. Sam and Josh looked nice in their dark grey suits and the younger girls wore light grey dresses. They would have looked a sight in their regular clothing. Now they seemed like a recycled family, but with no parents and a future that was still a mystery.

After the opening prayer, Christine read a passage from the Bible. Halfway though, her voice cracked and she stopped. The church was silent, except for the wall fans that spun in vain, trying to cool the congregation. Her eyes blurred and she blinked to clear them, aware that everybody was waiting for her to continue. She took a deep breath, stood tall and continued reading to the end of the verse.

"This is the word of the Lord."

She sniffed as the congregation responded, "Thanks be to God."

While she listened to the eulogy Aunt Celia gave, Christine discovered things about her father she hadn't known. He'd gone to agricultural college and won prizes at the parish fair for animal husbandry–whatever that was.

As Aunt Celia spoke about her brother, Christine realized she'd loved him as she said. She didn't cry as she reflected on their childhood in the village, but saved her tears for when she got back to her seat.

Christine tried hard to ignore the younger children's sniffling. Her mind went everywhere it had ever been on those trips Ma'am's beatings had forced her to take. Still, she kept straying into the present, her eyes drawn to the casket.

Aunt Celia sat and leaned against her husband's shoulder. Her son, Claude, blinked several times and looked at his fingers.

After the choir sang *How Great Thou Art,* drawing out the notes and making Christine feel worse, the family led the way to the graveside. Aunt Icy took Josh, Jamie and Cass back to her house, and went to finish the preparations for the customary funeral reception.

Christine and Sam stayed, but didn't take part in the singing by Daddy's grave. They both wept, hugging each other as the men lowered the casket into the oblong they had dug out of the dirt.

The priest said the last rites and threw a handful of soil, which hit the top of the coffin. Christine turned her head away, not wanting to see Daddy sealed away from her forever.

At the end, the grave-diggers covered the fresh rectangle of cement with a cluster of red, white, yellow and pink wreaths. In a way, Christine was relieved to have the funeral over and done with, but she worried that with his body inside the earth, the final cord to Daddy was cut.

He would be alone under the dirt while they moved on to what, she wasn't sure. She didn't talk to Sam on the ride to their temporary home. Instead, she prayed they would stay together.

Aunt Celia had told Aunt Icy that Ma'am would be moved to the sanitarium in Hoopersville. Though she couldn't ask questions since she'd been eavesdropping, Christine understood what that meant and thanked God for the break from Ma'am.

They approached Aunt Icy's house, sitting in the back of Aunt Celia's car, bumping gently over the uneven road. The afternoon had turned cool and dark and somewhere close by, a group of birds chirped as though they had urgent business to discuss.

Eyeing the back of Aunt Celia's head, Christine squared her shoulders, determined to find out what plans she'd made for them.

Somehow, she'd find a moment to talk to Aunt Celia before she went home.

Christine suspected that whatever their aunt decided wouldn't be suitable for the five of them. By the time she stepped inside the house, she'd planned what to say to her aunt.

She had been in suspense long enough and her questions couldn't wait.

Chapter 9

Christine searched the room until her gaze rested on Aunt Celia, who was talking with a tall man, wearing a suit. He looked familiar, but Christine couldn't say where she'd seen him before. It was hard to keep track of the people who attended the funeral; many recognized her, but sometimes she couldn't remember the names of those who spoke with her.

She stopped at her aunt's elbow. "Aunt Celia?"

"Yes?" She turned and looked at Christine.

"I need to talk to you."

Her aunt's brows drew down and Christine almost lost her nerve.

"Sure," Aunt Celia excused herself and touched Christine's shoulder.

The man she'd been talking to followed them with his eyes, and over her shoulder Christine watched him. She put him out of her mind as she led her aunt to her room in the Powell's house. Aunt Celia closed the door behind them, and they sat in two matching wicker chairs.

"What's on your mind?" Aunt Celia asked.

Christine stared at the embroidered pattern on her dress while gathering her courage. "I don't mean to be pushy, but I want to know what's going to happen to all of us."

"You're a bright girl, so you'll understand what I'm going to tell you." She smoothed the hair over her ears and took a deep breath. "Maxwell left a will. In it, he asked that I adopt you if anything happened to him. In fact—"

Ignoring everything Daddy had taught her about good manners, Christine stopped Aunt Celia. "But what about the younger ones?"

Aunt Celia rested a hand over Christine's fists. "I can't care for all of you. It would be impossible."

Christine leaned forward, intent on changing her aunt's mind. "Please, Aunt Celia. If you don't take us in, what will happen to Sam, Cass, Jamie and Josh? My mother's not coming back, is she?"

Shaking her head, Aunt Celia met Christine's eyes. "From what Maxwell told me and what I've seen, you're far more mature than your eleven years. You must understand that I can't do what you're asking?"

"Why can't they stay here with Aunt Icy?"

"Because it's up to the law to decide."

"But can't you ask Aunt Icy to keep them?"

"Things aren't that simple."

Christine pulled her hands from her aunt's grasp and dragged both fists over her eyes. Too near to tears to speak above a whisper, she asked, "What's going to happen to them?"

Aunt Celia looked away. "They'll have to go to a home."

"A home!" Christine got to her feet. "You mean, like a children's home?"

"Yes, there's no alternative. We have no close relatives. I don't know your mother's family and even if I did, I wouldn't..." Aunt Celia's voice trailed away.

Christine let the tears stream from her eyes. She was so tired of crying, not to mention angry that she couldn't think of anything to say to convince Aunt Celia they had to stay together. How could she be happy if she was separated from her family and how would they manage without her?

Christine tried again, talking around the pain in her throat. "Would you let me stay with them in the home?"

Aunt Celia shook her head. "I can't do that. You father left specific instructions. I can't go against his wishes. It would be against the law."

"So my brothers and sisters will be in a home and I get to live with you."

Aunt Celia rubbed her forehead with her fingertips. "I'm sorry, but that's the way it has to be."

Christine thought how strange it was that she had got her wish, but at the expense of her family.

She'd do anything to be able to go back and she'd put up with everything that came her way if it meant Daddy was alive. A simple wish to be away from Ma'am had cost them Daddy's life.

Ma'am was right, she was nothing but trouble.

Christine rested her arms on the chair and gazed at the ceiling. She wasn't sure why she was staring up there and looked down when her vision went hazy. She caught Aunt Celia looking at the ceiling, but was too worn out to smile. Aunt Celia twitched when Christine spoke. "What's going to happen to my mother?"

"Well, I can't say for sure. The doctors will decide if she's fit to stand trial for Max's..."

Aunt Celia put a hand to her throat as if the words were stuck there, and didn't finish what she started to say.

Christine didn't take her eyes off Aunt Celia as she swallowed, smoothed her hair and licked her lips. After she sucked in a deep breath, she tried again. "If she does stand trial, she might go to prison. If not, they'll keep her in the sanitarium for treatment."

Aunt Celia sat straighter, clasping her hands. "Let me ask you something. Say she is ever released, would you want your brothers and sisters to be in Ellie's care?"

Christine knew her expression said everything.

"I didn't think so," Aunt Celia said.

"This must seem like the end of the world to you. My brother adored you and I know you loved him." Her voice faded as they stared at each other.

She pressed her neck again before speaking. "The way things have worked out might be for the best. Not my brother's death, of course, but Ellie hasn't been right in her head for a long time. I told Max..."

She left the rest unsaid and Christine wondered what she was thinking. Aunt Celia's face twisted as if someone had pinched her hard, but her eyebrows smoothed out when she met Christine's gaze.

"When are we—" Christine corrected herself. "When are they going into the home and where is it?"

"Well, I was sure you'd want them close by, so I've contacted the nearest place of safety, which is in Downswell, an hour from my house. You can visit once each week. That won't be so bad, will it?"

"I don't know. We've always been together," Christine said, but her thoughts wouldn't settle. What if they didn't have enough to eat or what if someone abused them? There was talk about those things in the news sometimes. Christine shook her head, anxious over the images flooding her mind.

"You're just a child. You can't be responsible for what happens to your brothers and sisters," Aunt Celia said, patting her hand.

Christine pulled her hand away and straightened her back. "I've always taken care of them. I'm the oldest. You know that."

Aunt Celia bit her lip, but said nothing. She looked up when Christine spoke again. "There's something I have to know. Daddy wouldn't tell me and I can't ask him now."

She stared at her aunt, aware of the weight of her sadness pulling her mouth down at the corners.

Aunt Celia gripped the chair arms, frowning at Christine. "What is it?"

Christine swallowed a few times to get her voice working. "I think I'm the reason Ma'am killed Daddy—"

"I'm sure you're wrong."

"No, I'm not." She set her jaw to let Aunt Celia know she was serious. "Ma'am hates me. She's hated me forever."

Aunt Celia smoothed her hair again, although it was neat. The wind coming through the window made the only sound in the room. When Christine looked at Aunt Celia, she stared out the window as if she'd lost something in the yard. After some time, she cleared her throat and faced Christine. "What did you want to ask me?"

Christine held on to both sides of the cushion, determined to get the truth out of Aunt Celia. "Can you tell me why Ma'am hates me?"

Aunt Celia stopped moving, except for her gaze that bounced around the room and then hit the bed, dressing table and wardrobe. Christine cocked her head when Aunt Celia attempted to speak, but didn't say anything.

Christine raised her eyebrows to encourage Aunt Celia to talk. She pressed her lips together, her mouth opened, but only strange noises came out.

Christine wondered if Aunt Celia was going to be sick.

Chapter 10

Someone rapped at the door twice.

Christine hoped they would stop knocking and go away, but that didn't happen.

"Come in," Aunt Celia called.

The door opened and her husband held on to the knob. "We're almost ready to go," he said, glancing at Christine.

"Give me half an hour," Aunt Celia said, "remember I need to talk to the children."

"Okay, I'll be in the yard." Uncle Michael closed the door behind him and the sound of his footsteps faded as he walked away.

Christine hid her frustration, telling herself that at least she knew what was going to happen. Since she would be living with Auntie, she'd get answers to the questions tumbling over each other in her brain. She just had to be patient.

Aunt Celia got up and took Christine's hand. "I'll be back for you on Friday," she said, "Before I leave I'll tell your brothers and sisters what's going to happen. I'll talk to Aunt Icy and then see all of you in the living room."

She left, and Christine sank into the chair, dreading how her brothers and sisters would react to news of their separation.

When Christine entered to the living room, Sam, Cass, Jamie and Josh sat on the couches, still wearing their funeral clothes and looking as if they expected bad news.

Most of their neighbours who attended the funeral had eaten the Curried Goat dinner and left.

Aunt Icy passed Christine carrying a tray of food and told Aunt Celia she'd be in the backyard seeing to the few people who sat under the tent.

While Aunt Celia told Sam, Cass and Jamie they had to go live in the home, Christine slid lower in her seat. She stared at the whatnot, its inside crammed with cups, saucers, dishes and plates. On the H-shaped shelves, Aunt Icy had crowded figurines of birds and animals together on circular doilies.

"I wish things were different," Aunt Celia said, "but for now, this is the best I can do. D'you understand?"

Nobody said anything, but Sam scratched at his pants while Cass eyed Christine out of sides of her eyes, as if she couldn't wait to find out if what their Aunt said was true. Jamie sucked her thumb and Josh bounced his heels off the sofa.

Aunt Celia stood up and ran both hands over the front of her jacket. "Take care. I have to go now."

After she left, nobody was in the mood to talk, but Christine decided that in the time she had with them, she'd make sure they knew she'd come to visit. Josh wouldn't understand until they went to the home.

Over the next two days, Christine turned their coming move into a game. She quizzed them on what to do if anybody picked on them or if someone tried to hurt any of them. The guidance counselor at school did the same thing in class and told them that although they were young, they should be alert.

A make-believe session wasn't enough, but it was all Christine could think of, and it made her feel useful.

On Friday afternoon, when Aunt Celia arrived, Christine had everything packed, but was unwilling to go anywhere. She hoped that by a miracle, something had changed and they would all get to stay in the same place.

Before they left the house, Aunt Celia told Christine she had gone to the home the previous day.

"It's clean and the house-mothers seem kind. I think it will do," she said. "I also bought some things for all of you."

Christine had never been apart from her brothers and sisters any longer than the time they spent at school. Now, she sensed their fear of separation as clearly as she felt her own, but couldn't do anything to ease their minds.

While they filed out of the house to the yard, it occurred to Christine that it might be the last time they would be in one place as a family.

The Jeep was roomy enough to hold everybody and their luggage, so they travelled with Aunt Icy. Sam stared out the window, while Cass and Jamie sat on either side of Christine. She wished the ride would never end, but knew she'd soon have to face leaving her brothers and sisters.

Two towns away, down a side road, a worn-out sign announced their arrival at the Downswell Place of Safety. A guardhouse stood at the entrance of the property and a brick fence ran in both directions for what seemed like several miles. A man wearing a uniform came out and spoke to Aunt Celia, wrote her name down and then opened the gate.

On their way up the driveway, Christine counted at least six houses, where she figured the children slept. At the main building, they sat on wooden benches on the verandah, while Aunt Celia went into the office.

After what Christine thought must have been an hour, Aunt Celia came back with a woman as round and short as Aunt Icy. She had grey hair and crinkles around her eyes when she smiled.

"I'm Mrs. Bernice James, but you can call me Auntie B," she said. "We're going to show you where you'll be staying."

Auntie B got inside Aunt Celia's car and the children followed in the Jeep with Aunt Icy. They drove for less than two minutes before they pulled up at another building. After they got out, Auntie B explained that Cass and Jamie would live there, and Sam and Josh would be housed on a separate building for boys.

Christine helped take the girls' bags to a room with four beds that Aunt B showed them. Christine wasn't sure what to expect, but was happy her sisters didn't have to share space with a whole bunch of other children.

The bedroom was large and painted in pale green. A small chest-of-drawer rested beside each bed and a huge dresser with a mirror stood against the far wall, close to a set of grilled, double windows. The white terrazzo tiles made the room seem spacious. The bedroom was better than the one they shared at home and Cass and Jamie had their own beds. Sweet.

Christine helped them unpack and reminded Cass to take care of their things.

Auntie B came back to the room when they were almost finished, bringing Aunt Celia and two girls she introduced as Cass and Jamie's roommates. Jennifer was tall and skinny and wore glasses and Marie was plump and friendly. Both girls waved at Cass and Jamie and said hello.

Christine filed their names away in her mind, thinking they looked as if they would get along okay with her sisters. The girls ran off when Auntie B told them they could go. Aunt Celia, Christine and her sisters followed Auntie B back the way they had come.

While Christine hugged Cass and Jamie, Sam sat on the wall enclosing the verandah and stared into the yard. Josh sat close by, playing with his airplane. Christine went to sit with Sam, pulling Cass and Jamie with her. She touched his shoulder and when he raised his head, his eyes shone.

"You're in charge now, Sam. You have to take care of them."

He nodded and wiped away the tears trickling to his chin. He hardly ever cried, which made Christine want to cry too. Auntie stood in the doorway talking to Auntie B, but she kept an eye on them. Squeezing Cass and Jamie to her, Christine reminded them she'd see them soon.

Auntie came over and patted Cass, Jamie and Sam on the shoulder. "We have to go now."

Aunt Icy, who'd waited on the verandah, hugged each of them and promised to visit. Josh tried to follow Christine down the steps, but Sam grabbed his arm. Screaming his frustration, Josh covered his eyes with the back of one arm, while flapping the other to get away from Sam, who held him tight.

Aunt Icy got in the Jeep, blowing her nose in a hanky she pulled out of her skirt.

Taking Christine's hand firmly, Aunt Celia opened the door and made her get inside the car. As they drew away from the building, Christine knelt in the back seat, gazing at her brothers and sisters.

They stood close together, arms around each other. Their shapes wobbled and formed one big blob as Christine's tears came. She sat when the car reached the main road, looking away from Aunt Celia who watched her through the rear view mirror.

Christine was grateful Aunt Celia didn't try to talk to her or tell her things would get better.

On Christine's side of the car, the tree trunks in the woodland whizzed by and were the only things she recognized. It was like looking at a painting with the bright colours removed. She imagined that Sam and the others felt worse. She closed her eyes, hoping their first night in their new home wouldn't be unbearable.

When the car slowed and they entered a housing scheme with cement buildings on individual lots of land, Christine stirred. The plants and flowers in many of the yards were neat, as if the owners spent hours taking care of them.

Butterflies fluttered around blooms in pink, white, yellow and more colours than Christine had ever seen in any place at once.

Aunt Celia took several turns before they pulled into the driveway of one of the yards.

Christine stared at the house and her mouth opened. Aunt Celia's home was nothing like she'd imagined.

It was better.

Chapter 11

After showing Christine around the house, Aunt Celia took her to a bedroom with a double bed, a desk and dresser. The yellow curtains splashed with daisies matched the sheet and pillow cases. When Aunt Celia said the room was hers, tears flooded Christine's eyes. If only Cass and Jamie could share it with her.

"Where are Uncle Michael and Claude?" Christine asked, while looking around.

"They'll be here in another half hour or so. Claude has Karate. Go ahead and unpack. I'll check on you in a bit."

Christine put some of her things in the dresser drawer and then lay on the bed. She closed her eyes, rubbing her cheek against the sheets. Boy, they smelled nice and fresh.

Her smile disappeared when she remembered the last glimpse she'd had of her brothers and sisters. A knock sounded on the door and Christine sighed and sat up.

"Come in."

She cleared her throat, realizing she'd whispered. She wasn't used to anyone asking permission to enter her room. Ma'am always barged in instead of knocking. She spoke again, this time louder. "Come in!"

"Everything all right?" Aunt Celia asked.

Christine nodded. "Yes."

Aunt Celia sat on the bed facing Christine, who pressed her hands together and stared at them.

"It's not your fault, you know," Aunt Celia said.

"What?" Christine asked, examining her knuckles.

"Everything that's happened."

"Well, my mother says it is."

Aunt Celia touched her shoulder. "Sometimes adults have problems that they don't handle very well."

"Are you talking about Ma'am's mental problems?"

Auntie's eyes opened wider, but she nodded and continued, "And they say hurtful things. Aunt Icy told me what your mother said to you when the police arrested her."

Christine played with a bit of thread on her skirt, sitting up straight when Aunt Celia came closer and put an arm around her shoulder. She didn't want to move away, which might make Aunt Celia feel bad, but she wasn't comfortable being so close to her.

"Like I said, this isn't your fault. Max and your mother had problems." Aunt Celia sighed and her voice went low as if she was talking to herself. "They shouldn't have been together in the first place."

Christine raised her head, wanting to find out more, but Auntie's frown said she had given away too much. Sighing again, she squeezed Christine's shoulder. "Your mother and I didn't see eye to eye on a lot of things."

"Daddy did tell me the two of you didn't get along."

"We didn't, but I had to respect the choices my brother made."

"How did Daddy meet my mother?"

Aunt Celia licked her lips and squinted as though looking into the past. "They met one Christmas when they both came home for the holidays."

"Did they fall in love?"

Aunt Celia chuckled and patted Christine's hand. "You either read a lot or you've watched more television than is good for you, but based on what Max told me, I'd say you're well read."

She smiled again. "Your Mom did love my brother in the beginning. I also believe she liked the idea of being in love. Max was a handsome fellow and the girls in Sheaville were all a little in love with him."

Her voice trailed off and seconds passed before she continued. "Then, he met Ellie."

Christine tipped her head sideways, frowning because Aunt Celia sounded as if she was talking about two different persons. She didn't say anything for a few minutes and her lips trembled as if she was going to cry.

To take Aunt Celia's mind off things, Christine asked a question. "You didn't get to answer what I asked about my mother."

Aunt Celia stared at her, eyebrows rumpled. "Ah, yes. I don't believe your mother hates you, but like I said, Ellie has deep issues and sometimes..."

"Daddy would tell me the truth," Christine said.

Aunt Celia walked to the window, leaned against the frame and stared into the yard. Her brow wrinkled like Daddy's, when he was thinking.

Aunt Celia's shoulders lifted and fell as she took a deep breath, which Christine heard from where she sat. Auntie folded and unfolded her arms and then walked back to Christine.

"A lot has happened in the past week and you've gone through many changes. I'm not sure how much I can or should tell you. Although you're mature, you're just a little girl. There are things you can't possibly understand."

"Daddy said that too."

"And I don't think now is the time—"

Christine narrowed her eyes. Adults made long speeches when they wanted to avoid answering questions. What didn't Auntie want her to find out?

Without meaning to, she held on to Aunt Celia's wrist. "I've been thinking about this since Daddy died."

Conscious of her hold on her aunt's arm, Christine let go, but continued speaking. "Will you promise to tell me the truth if I tell you what I think?"

Two short lines appeared between Aunt Celia's brows. She was thinking again. After a long stretch of time, Aunt Celia nodded, but didn't seem happy.

Christine sucked in some air and looked into her aunt's eyes. "I look like you and Daddy. My mother didn't like it and said so all the time. She said I was ugly like him."

The lines on Aunt Celia's forehead went deeper.

"Cass, Jamie, Sam and Josh resemble each other and I only look like them a little bit. How come?"

Her aunt took a few steps back, which brought her to the window. She breathed hard as if she'd just finished a race, but Christine's questions were too important for her to stop now.

"You know what I think, Aunt Celia?"

Auntie didn't answer, but reached for the window ledge with one hand. With the other, she felt for the crucifix at her throat. Both hands trembled and she swallowed hard.

"I don't think my real mother is the one I know. You know why?"

Auntie's lips parted as if she wanted to say something, but Christine didn't give her a chance.

"I don't look anything like Ma'am and I'm too old. My parents had their tenth anniversary this year and I'm all of eleven plus. *And…*" Christine stopped, pleased with her logic.

"I've been thinking about this even before Daddy died." Squinting as she shared her thoughts, she continued, "Ma'am hates it when Daddy and I spend time together."

Christine realized she was speaking about Daddy as if he was still alive, and now that she had the freedom to tell someone how Ma'am had treated her, the words wouldn't stop coming.

"Although Ma'am hits the others sometimes, she never slaps them as hard. And she has a weird way of looking at me. She never ever hugged me. Well, not that I can remember."

Christine shook her head and got up to stand in front of Aunt Celia. She waited a few seconds before she spoke. "Tell me the truth. Is Ma'am my birth mother?"

Auntie's eyes flew open to twice their usual size. She looked like Sam did whenever Christine caught him doing something wrong. Aunt Celia cleared her throat, let out her breath and drew it in again. She shut her eyes and her face cleared. When her eyelids opened, Christine didn't move or breathe.

"No, Christine, she isn't," Aunt Celia said, looking over Christine's shoulder.

Christine's shoulders drooped, but she wasn't unhappy. She'd expected Auntie to lie and was shocked that she hadn't. What a relief to have her suspicion confirmed. Just like that. If she'd known it would have been this easy, she'd have asked way earlier.

A grin seized Christine's face and she bounced to the bed and sat on the edge, whispering. "I was right all along. I knew it!"

Chapter 12

Celia stood in the kitchen, slicing tomatoes to add to the salad. In her mind's eye, she saw Christine's face. Looking into her eyes was like staring at Max; it was almost spooky, and brought a host of questions flooding into Celia's head space.

The one first on the list was where an eleven-year-old would have heard the term 'birth mother'? It wasn't one people used in casual conversation, which meant Christine had done some research.

As a teacher, Celia knew it was a mistake to underestimate any child, but Christine had floored her by being vocal about her life and the information she needed.

Nausea settled in Celia's stomach over revealing facts Max and Ellie had chosen to bury. Christine's pleading and persuasiveness had slipped past Celia's defenses and made her divulge something she hadn't intended to, and which wasn't her business.

All sorts of backlash would come from talking out of turn. Christine wasn't likely to stop digging and the more questions she thought of, the more difficult it would be to answer them.

If she was my mother, she'd love me.

Christine's words carried simple conviction and had come after Celia asked what made her think Ellie wasn't her mother.

The circumstances surrounding her birth and how she came to be with Maxwell and Ellie weren't easy to understand. Celia anticipated a hard couple of weeks ahead, trying to explain those facts to a child as young as Christine, no matter her level of maturity.

Celia finished making the salad, cleaned the counter and then stood by the window. She rubbed the crucifix on her necklace, the familiar pattern of the grooves and ridges bringing comfort to her anxious mind.

Her words could not be reversed, but she could prepare for the emotional turmoil to come, knowing Christine would need her support.

Had she betrayed Max by revealing his secret? How would she get Christine to understand the past without being devastated?

Despite warning herself not to worry, Celia wondered if she had made a terrible mistake.

Celia sat propped up in bed, a book open on her lap. Michael lay snoring with his back to her. She poked him gently. "Michael?"

"Hmmm?"

"Christine wants to talk to James," she said.

"Who's James?"

"Her uncle. Jimmy," Celia said, brushing aside her impatience. Michael rolled over, frowning. "Is that wise?"

Having discussed Max's situation with Michael over the years, he was aware of her brother's wishes regarding Christine.

Celia had confessed to him that she'd disclosed information about Max during the marathon question and answer session with Christine earlier in the day.

Celia massaged her brow and sighed. "The fact that she has an uncle kinda slipped out."

Michael sat up and faced her. "Well, there's no point hiding anything from her. She's handled everything well so far, considering..."

Flipping the pages of the book, Celia shared the thoughts bouncing back and forth in her head. "D'you think I've done the right thing, telling her the truth? It's a matter of time before she asks about her mother. What do I tell her then?"

Michael's indulgent expression comforted her. His concerned gaze and ready smile under his neat moustache reminded her of the reasons she loved him.

"I think you're taking the best approach. What's that you tell Claude?" He scratched his head. "Speak the truth and speak it ever, cost it what it will?"

She nodded. "Yeah, but sometimes it sounds a lot easier than it actually is."

"True that." Michael lay down again, wriggling a few times to get comfortable. Celia's mind continued to hum with thoughts surrounding Christine.

"Michael?"

"Hmm?"

"You really believe what I've done is best?"

Michael yawned, sat up again and put his arm around her. "Yes, I do. Christine's a bit skittish—as if she expects us to hit her at any moment, but I guess that's because of Ellie's treatment. Otherwise, from what I see, she seems okay."

He stroked Celia's shoulder and continued speaking. "You've been handling children for a long time and have always said the truth is much simpler to handle. Why change your mind now? I know I asked a minute ago if allowing her to talk to her uncle was wise, but I don't doubt that you will make the right decision."

She fussed with the edges of the book, stroking the pages. "She's had a hard life and I don't want to do or say anything to make things worse."

Michael said nothing for a while and when he spoke, sounded as though he was choosing his words with care. "I look at Christine and beneath her shyness, I see a strong little girl. She'll be okay. She has character."

"I know," Celia said.

"Don't worry. She can't go wrong. She has you for an aunt, remember?"

He chucked her under the chin. "Besides, if you can't handle one child after all these years of being a teacher, then I don't know who can."

"I just wish I was as confident about this as you seem to be."

Michael pecked her on the cheek. "Stop worrying. It isn't going to change anything. Some sleep will do you good," he said.

She put the book aside, turned off the bedside lamp and stared at the curtains. Long after Michael fell asleep, she lay awake listening to his breath whistling in and out past his clogged sinuses. Sleep was a long time coming for her.

Chapter 13

Christine used a garden shovel to dig around the roots of the Ixora, careful not to go too deep.

She had learnt all sorts of interesting things in the days since she moved to Auntie's home. She knew how to make Sweet and Sour Sauce and Auntie had started teaching her Crochet. Today she was showing her how to care for the garden.

Auntie gave the mound of dirt around the Rain Lily she'd planted a final tease with the shovel. She tipped her head up to look at Christine. "You finished?"

"Yes. See?" Christine pointed to the tilled soil under the row of green and gold Duranta, a proud grin in place.

When Auntie stood, her knee clicked. She grunted and then chuckled while removing her gardening gloves. "My joints are telling me I'm not as young as I used to be."

"Forty-five isn't very old," Christine said, thinking Auntie only looked old when she scrunched up her face.

Patting Christine's shoulder, Auntie said, "You're a good girl, you know that?"

Christine sighed. "Ma'am doesn't think so."

They moved to sit on the wooden bench in the shade of the Mango tree, where Aunt Celia took off her floppy hat and smoothed her hair. The grey streaks raised a question in Christine's mind. "Auntie, how come Claude is so young?"

Auntie laughed, shaking her head. "Don't you mean you think I'm too old to be the mother of a boy his age?

"I spent my dating years studying and missed all the fun stuff. When I met Michael, I was in my thirties," she said.

Christine digested that while sadness crept over her. "Maybe if Daddy had waited, he'd have found..."

Auntie rested a hand on Christine's shoulder. "About your Uncle Jimmy—"

"Yes?"

"D'you want to talk to him this week? I think he leaves the island again soon."

Christine slapped her palms together. Meeting someone connected to her mother would be really cool. "Yes, please!"

Aunt Celia scraped her bottom lip with her teeth. "Remember the things I promised to tell you? Questions I didn't answer the other day."

Christine nodded. "Uh-huh."

Aunt Celia's sober face did nothing to curb Christine's excitement.

"It's about your mom and dad."

Christine leaned forward, almost on her feet.

Aunt Celia touched Christine's cheek before folding her hands together. "Up to ten years ago, if a girl got pregnant around these parts, people said she was bad. They were raised to believe that good girls got married before they had children."

Christine studied Auntie, while grabbing blades of grass between her toes.

"So when my mommy had me, people thought she was bad?"

"Some did. Sometimes people talk about others and the things they say can make life uncomfortable, especially if they think you've made a mistake."

"So, I was a mistake?" Christine asked, frowning.

"No, Christine. I didn't say that."

Christine went silent. She knew exactly how neighbours talked from the times she'd gone to town with Ma'am. People looked at them as if they were from another planet, which was embarrassing, and they stopped talking when Christine and Ma'am got close. Christine always felt they were gossiping about them, and Ma'am's way of dressing didn't help.

The few times Ma'am had gone to school on Parent/Teacher Consultation Day, Christine saw the difference between Ma'am and the other mothers. They dressed in nice clothes and had neat hairstyles, while Ma'am always wore a tie-head and a dress that looked as if it belonged to someone two sizes bigger. The main thing that set her apart though, was her habit of telling her children bad words. Christine got the worst of it, and Ma'am cursed anywhere.

Christine closed her eyes, glad those days were over. Her mind settled on her brothers and sisters and she hoped they were doing all right. She looked up when Auntie touched her hand.

"Your mother was in her first year of teacher's college when she got pregnant with you."

"So she was going to be a teacher like you?"

"Yes, but I think she believed she couldn't be a good mother to you, and continue with her schooling at the same time."

"So that's how Daddy ended up raising me?"

"Yes, remember how I told you that sometimes we make difficult choices that hurt other people?"

Christine nodded.

"Well, your mother decided to leave you with your dad."

"You mean she didn't want me?" Christine whispered as hot, painful tears started in her eyes.

"I wouldn't say that." Auntie hugged Christine to her side. "Your grandparents didn't approve of my brother. Although Max was willing to marry Roma, her parents wouldn't allow it. They had plans to migrate and your mother's pregnancy complicated things."

She paused and gently tugged one of Christine's plaits. "Are you with me so far?"

Christine bobbed her head.

"They had to shelve their plans for a year because they didn't want to leave Roma. They waited for you to be born and a few months after you came, Roma gave you to your father."

"Just like that?" Christine pressed the heels of her hands over both eyes to stop the tears.

"She didn't want to leave you, but she felt she had no choice. As much as she loved Max, she wasn't strong enough to go against her parents' wishes."

Hurt and confusion swirled inside Christine. The woman she thought was her mother had never loved her. Now she had a real, live mother who hadn't thought enough of her to stay in Jamaica. Something had to be wrong with her. If none of her two mothers loved her, how did Auntie feel about her?

She decided to ask.

"If Daddy had asked you to let me stay with you, would you have said yes?"

Auntie's answer was quick. "You're a gem, and my brother wouldn't have asked for help if he didn't need it. So that's a yes. I'm surprised he allowed you to go through what you did with Ellie, and didn't deal with it sooner."

Christine squinted at her, and Auntie spoke after a moment. "Aunt Icy told me about some of the things that used to happen."

Christine hastened to defend her father. "Daddy tried to be home as much as possible and he didn't leave me alone with Ma'am unless he had to."

"I understand," Aunt Celia said. "Anyway, I'm glad you came to live with us. We can get to do all the fun stuff mothers and daughters do together."

"Really?"

"Really," Auntie said, giving her another squeeze.

"Auntie? One more thing."

Aunt Celia raised her brows and tilted her head toward Christine.

"Would you give me a little more time to decide if I want to meet my uncle? I'm not so sure I want to see him again, or to know anything more about my mother."

She blinked hard, trying not to cry. "I don't understand how I have two mothers and not one of them is interested in me."

She held both hands out as if begging for understanding.

"Christine, it's not that simple."

"It is to me," Christine said, shoving Auntie's arm off her shoulder.

She ran inside, going by instinct as the tears flooding her eyes made it impossible for her to see anything.

Chapter 14

C elia stared after Christine, wondering if she'd lost her mind when she chose to tell her niece the truth about her parents.

Even if she'd done it in a moment of madness, it was too late to turn back now. She cursed herself for the compulsion she felt to be honest, no matter the situation. Not that beating up herself made any sense.

Sure, she could have avoided revealing everything she knew, but wouldn't that have done more harm than good?

Celia's job had taught her that children did much better if parents helped to build their self-esteem. She'd seen too many young people damaged by careless words and thoughtless actions.

With Christine in her care, the responsibility fell to Celia to nurture her and that included letting her know she was important, although her early history suggested otherwise.

While questioning her decision, Celia's hand went to the crucifix. "God, what have I done?" she whispered.

Though she tried to reassure herself she'd done what a good guardian would do, she had serious doubts about her actions.

If only Max had listened to her, but he'd always been stubborn, more so if he thought he was doing the right thing. Eleven years ago he'd taken the course of action he figured was best for Christine, but tunnel vision had resulted in his murder.

Celia sighed and rubbed a hand over her eyes. She wouldn't forgive herself if their family secrets caused Christine permanent damage.

Chapter 15

On Saturday afternoon, Christine joined Aunt Celia in the backyard, watching while she pampered the plants. That's what she said the last time Christine asked what she was doing.

Christine ran her fingers over a peach Hibiscus bloom, gazing at the flowers that crowded each other in a whirl of pink, red, white and yellow. The backyard was a sea of colour from the ground to the shade of the trees where Auntie's orchids hung in wire baskets lined with coir.

"Ma'am won't be back for a long time, right?"

Although she thought she knew the answer, Christine wanted to be sure Ma'am wouldn't come to take her home. At the same time, she felt sick wondering what might be happening to Josh, Jamie, Cass and Sam. She forced herself to pay attention to Auntie's answer.

"No, even if she's not fit to go to court, it will be a while before they release her from the asylum. Plus, I'm now your legal guardian, remember?"

Christine allowed that to sink in before she asked the next question. "What's wrong with her?"

"She suffers from severe depression. The medical term these days is Bipolar Disorder."

"Is that why she treated me like she did?"

"I suppose. She would have had mood swings because of her illness. You know, one moment she'd be doing normal stuff and the next, she'd be sad or angry."

"*I know* it was more than that," Christine said.

She spun the bloom between her fingers, her mind straying again to the home and how her brothers and sisters were doing on their own. She shifted on the bench and tilted her head back when the Mango leaves rustled in the warm breeze that brushed her skin.

Christine hugged herself, still cherishing the knowledge that she had a mother, apart from Ma'am. Many times, she'd asked herself how Ma'am could beat her as if she hated her.

Over the years, Ma'am had said things to make Christine feel stupid, ugly and worthless. Then, she remembered Daddy, who'd always told her how much he loved her.

Auntie pressed her thumb over the mouth of the hose, which hissed while she sprinkled the roots of the plants. She had to be wondering why Christine had stopped asking about her real mother.

It wasn't that Christine didn't want to find out, but Auntie had proven she could be trusted. She'd had the chance to lie about Christine's birth mother, but she didn't. Christine respected her for that.

Auntie turned off the water, curled the hose over the pipe and came to sit beside Christine. "How exactly did Ellie treat you?"

"She didn't like having me around." Christine laid the bloom aside and picked at the hem of her skirt. "She beat me for everything, even things I didn't do."

She remembered Daddy telling Ma'am on the day he died that she took everything out on her.

"It got so bad, I asked Daddy if he would send me to stay with you."

Auntie rubbed her hands together, but didn't speak.

"That's what started the last argument," Christine said.

"You don't know that for sure," Auntie said, touching her arm. "Remember I told you not blame yourself for any of that."

A few minutes went by before Christine asked another question. "How long ago did Daddy make you my guardian?"

"When he made his will two months ago."

Christine chewed that over before she spoke, her tone gloomy. "D'you think he knew he was going to die?"

Auntie curled her fingers around Christine's hand. "I really don't know, but he was certain he wanted you to be with me and I'm happy to have you."

"Go watch some television," Aunt Celia said after a moment, and got to her feet.

Christine figured Auntie was trying to prevent her from thinking too much and maybe getting upset. Christine was glad for that. It was cooler inside anyway.

While she stared at the television screen, Christine thought she'd soon be spoiled rotten. Claude, who was twelve and addicted to cartoons, kept his gaze glued to the set. Every few minutes, he laughed at the animated characters who clowned around trying to find a missing squirrel. Christine caught herself giggling, still amazed that Claude was free to laugh without anyone telling him to shut up and turn down the television.

A crackling sound reminded her that Uncle Michael sat in one corner, reading the newspapers. A small pile of papers lay on the floor beside him. When she tried to move them that morning, Claude had told her that his father saved the daily papers and caught up on the news on the weekend.

Christine's attention returned to the screen, but it wasn't long before her mind wandered. At home, Daddy didn't allow them to watch television on weekdays, but their reading was unrestricted. Christine wasn't used to sitting around doing nothing, but didn't want to get up and leave without permission.

She counted the huge yellow flowers on the drape, the figurines on the whatnot, the pictures on the wall and the blooms in the arrangement on the centre table.

"You don't have to stay if you don't want to," Uncle Michael said, lowering the papers. "You're free to do something else if you like."

Christine got up, grateful to escape. "Thanks."

Uncle Michael's smile served as his reply before he disappeared behind the newspaper.

Christine was ready to talk. The glow of discovery was wearing thin, so it was time to find out more about her mother.

On Sunday morning, she helped Aunt Celia in the kitchen. Their dinner menu was what most Jamaicans ate on a Sunday afternoon—Fried Chicken, Rice and Peas cooked in coconut milk, Potato Salad and vegetables. Christine's mouth watered at the lovely smells.

Ma'am had given up on preparing regular Sunday dinner, saying they couldn't afford meat every week or that she couldn't cook because her head was killing her.

When she had one of her headaches, she'd lie down all day. Christine always found it strange that Ma'am's headaches set in on Friday nights and lasted for two whole days, leaving Christine to run the house on weekends.

Daddy wasn't a good cook, so most of the time, they had sardines or Corned Beef with bread or crackers. Sometimes, Aunt Icy sent over enamel containers filled with tasty French Fried Chicken or slices of Roast Beef. Christine dragged her thoughts away from food and turned to the questions she needed to have answered.

"How well did you know my mother?"

Auntie hesitated before she answered. "Not very well."

Her hand slowed while she stirred the gravy on the stove. "We saw each other mostly on weekends since we went to the same church. She lived here, in Hoopersville and we lived in Sheaville. I'm ten years older than her, so we weren't very friendly."

"How did she meet Daddy?"

"That's hard to say. I'd guess in school. She was a few years younger than Max. They met again when she was in teacher's college and he was in agricultural school."

"D'you remember what she was like?"

Aunt Celia dropped the spoon in the sink before she answered. "She was pretty. You look a little like her, but a lot more like Max." She smiled and continued. "I remember her as kind and caring, and she adored Max."

"If she cared and loved Daddy, how come she isn't here?" Christine said, unable to hide her resentment.

Auntie wrung out the dishrag and wiped the counter. "Sometimes our choices hurt other people. It was like that with your mother."

"I sort of feel Daddy and I lived alone at some point."

"Who told you that?" Auntie asked, still cleaning the countertop.

"Nobody, and I don't *know* for sure. But I've had a feeling. You know how sometimes you remember something, but you're not sure it happened?"

Aunt Celia nodded while Christine leaned against the sink and folded her arms.

"I remember Daddy and me, together, without the others. It feels right, like it actually happened, but then I feel guilty about not wanting them around. I figured it might be my imagination. So, it was true, then?"

"Yes, you and Max were on your own for a time after our parents died. Mama used to take care of you during the days." She nudged Christine aside, washed out the rag and hung it on the edge of the sink before speaking again. "I'm amazed you remember that far back."

"Me too." Christine frowned. "Did she have parents? My mother, I mean."

"Of course." Aunt Celia rolled her eyes at Christine. "Remember I told you they all migrated together?"

"I forgot." Christine giggled at Auntie's eye-rolling. "What were they like?"

"I hardly knew them. Like I said, they didn't like the fact that their daughter had a relationship with Max."

Folding her arms, Christine stood straight. "Why?"

"They thought she was too good for my brother. Anyway..." Aunt Celia waved a hand, dismissing that thought.

"You said her name was Roma, right?"

"Yes. Roma Wint."

"Roma." Christine tested it on her tongue, eyes half closed. "So where do her parents live now?"

Aunt Celia walked over to the island in the middle of the room, picked up a folded towel and laid it open on the tiles.

"I guess they'd still be in Canada."

Christine's shoulders drooped at that bit of news.

"Just as I was thinking..." Christine's voice trailed off.

Auntie Celia hadn't done anything with the towel, but folded it again. "Tell me what's going on."

"I was looking forward to meeting my other family, but now I find out I don't have any."

Auntie's fingers crept to her crucifix. Christine's gaze sharpened. Although she had known Auntie for a short time, it was long enough to know she only fiddled with the pendant when she got worried or nervous. Christine turned to see what Auntie was looking at over her shoulder and realized she was thinking.

The silence stretched until Christine was sure Auntie didn't remember she was standing in the kitchen. She stared at Christine so long she began to fidget.

Holding on to Christine's shoulder, Auntie said, "D'you remember the man I was talking to after Max's funeral?"

Christine let her head sway back and forth. She wished she could remember because she sensed something important was coming.

Her aunt jogged her memory. "At Aunt Icy's house when you asked to talk to me?"

"You mean the one in the suit?"

Aunt Celia nodded and took a deep breath. "He's your mother's brother. The uncle you want to meet."

Christine's heart galloped and she wanted to whoop and holler. She hoped Aunt Celia wouldn't think she was ungrateful, but she was so happy there was a family out there that belonged to her. She even forgot her resentment over not being told her mother's true identity. Surely, her uncle must have more information about her mother.

A flash of guilt dimmed her excitement. Daddy had taken good care of her, but she couldn't deny the thrill of having a real mother; one who might love her.

Christine looked up at Auntie, who turned her head away. Her eyes were shiny, as if she wanted to cry. Christine put out a hand but drew it back. "Auntie, what's wrong?"

"Nothing. I don't want you to build up your hopes too much."

"I just want to know more about her. You're still going to let me talk to him now that I've made up my mind, right?"

Auntie took her time before answering. "Yes, but I'll be there with you, of course."

Aunt Celia picked up the towel and laid it in the drawer. She took another deep breath and then looked Christine in the eyes. "Before that happens, we must talk about a few things."

Christine was too excited to care that the lines reappeared in Auntie's forehead or that she was blinking again as if she couldn't hold back tears.

Chapter 16

J immy Wint examined Christine as closely as she studied him.
Christine couldn't find any family resemblance, but guessed from the slight frown and then a gradual smile that stretched to cover his face, he saw something that satisfied him.

Christine drew her hands over her skirt to dry her palms, looking to Auntie for help. Auntie squeezed her hand and smiled, letting her know everything was okay. Her uncle was sweating too, which made Christine relax a little.

Her need to know more about the woman who left her behind for a new life was stronger than Christine's resentment over being abandoned. That was why she decided to meet her mother's brother.

Auntie had contacted her uncle and he agreed to visit. Now he sat in their living room looking as uncomfortable as she felt. His large hands tapped the sofa's armrests and he couldn't stop looking at her.

"Can I get you something to drink, Jimmy?" Aunt Celia asked.

"Thanks."

Auntie got up and left the room, unaware of Christine's wordless plea for her to stay. They sat in silence, because Christine did not have the first clue where to begin asking questions.

"I went to your father's funeral," he said.

"I know. I saw you at Aunt Icy's house. Did you know about me then?"

He nodded. "Yes. You look like her."

Christine bit the inside of her lip to smother her smile.

Her uncle gazed around the room before asking, "D'you miss him?"

"Yes." Christine answered politely, though his question was silly. All the same, the mention of Daddy made her ready to cry.

Uncle Jimmy looked at his hands, rubbing them together as if he didn't know what to do with them.

Swallowing a few times, Christine tried not to shame herself and bawl like a baby. After she cleared her throat, she asked him the first thing that came to mind. "How is my mother?"

"She's okay," he said.

"Does she have any other children?"

His head jerked up and he squinted, surprised by her question. "Yes, two boys."

One side of his mouth curved in a teensy smile. "You're inquisitive. You remind me of her."

Christine couldn't hide her grin. "How old are they?" she asked.

"Five and seven."

Christine considered this and remembered something else she wanted to find out. "Is she married?"

Again, he looked surprised. She bet he was wondering why she needed to know.

"Yes, her husband's name is Charles."

Christine pleated the end of her skirt. "D'you think she ever thinks about me?"

For all his staring since they'd met, Jimmy Wint examined her as though seeing her for the first time.

"I'm sure she does," he said, speaking just above a whisper.

"D'you live in Canada too?"

"Half the time," he said and smiled again, showing nice teeth. He looked just like an uncle should.

"I live there six months of the year. The other six months, I spend here," he said, "give or take a few trips."

"Where's your family?" Christine asked.

He looked as if someone had jabbed him with a pin, and his smile disappeared. "Here and there."

The frown that fell over his face stopped Christine from asking any further questions.

Auntie returned, carrying a tray with three glasses of lemonade, which she set on the centre table.

"Thanks," Uncle Jimmy said after Aunt Celia handed him one of the frosty glasses.

Christine echoed her uncle when Auntie gave her a glass. The ice cubes clinked together, making a wonderful sound.

Christine hid a smile, thinking how much things had changed. A few weeks ago, it was out of the question for any adult to serve her. Ma'am always demanded whatever she wanted and Christine had to do as she was told. It was that, or risk a slap for not moving fast enough.

She wondered how Ma'am was doing. Her brothers and sisters also came to mind, but she'd think about them later. For the moment, she had other things to sort out, so she got ready to question Jimmy Wint again. "When are you going back to Canada?"

"In another couple of days."

"You'll be seeing my..." Christine hesitated, "her, when you get back?"

He nodded.

"D'you think she would mind getting a letter from me?"

"I have no idea," he said, his voice lower than before.

"Why did you agree to come?"

Her aunt and uncle looked at each other and then at her. Jimmy put both hands on his knees and took a while to answer.

"Well, I saw you at Max's funeral and since you resemble Roma a bit, I figured who you were.

"I was curious, so I asked Celia about you," he continued. "I don't know how Roma will react to hearing from you, but I'll take your letter to her. I still would have told her that I'd seen you, and I know she'll be sad to hear Maxwell died. He meant a lot to her."

While the possibility that her mother might not want to hear from her made Christine weepy, she held back a nasty smile. She was certain her uncle had seen it, but wouldn't know what she'd been thinking.

How special could her mother's feelings have been for her father, to run away and leave him to care for a baby by himself? She had a hundred other questions and not much time, so she decided to get on with the important ones.

"Is she a teacher?" she asked.

Her uncle nodded.

"What does she look like?"

He eased up on one side and pulled something out of his pocket. Christine sat on the edge of the cushion. This was too good to be true. Her eyes never left him as he flipped through his wallet. When he found what he was looking for, he held it out to her.

With her jaw hanging open, Christine got up and took the wallet. She sat, feeling just as she did at church during meditation time after Communion.

The two people in the picture smiled at her. She glanced up to make sure the man looking at her was the same one in the photo. When she was sure, she only had eyes for her mother.

Roma wore her hair in a ponytail, and Christine thought she did look a tad bit like her. Her mother's smile was pretty. As Christine stared into her mother's eyes, her own filled. She pushed the wallet toward her uncle, faster than she had planned and it fell to the floor.

She mumbled an apology, grabbed the wallet and shoved it into his hands. If it was possible, she'd have looked at the photograph all day. Instead, she let her gaze roam the room, stopping at each familiar item. She begged and pleaded for the heat in her eyes to go away. It wouldn't do for her to cry and make herself look stupid, so she twisted her fingers in her lap, reaching for some happy thoughts. Not one of them came to mind.

The sofa sank, but she refused to raise her head. Musky cologne, like the kind Uncle Michael wore, filled her nose. Her uncle sat and put something in her hand. She looked at a watery version of her mother's face.

Clearing his throat, he said, "I want you to have it."

"Really?" She turned to her aunt, forgetting her tears. "Can I keep it, Auntie?"

Auntie nodded.

"Won't you need it?" Christine asked, wiping her cheeks with the back of her hand.

Her uncle shook his head. "You have more use for it than I do. I can get one made from Roma's copy."

Uncle Jimmy patted her hand and got up. "I'll come by on Friday to collect that letter."

"Thanks," she said, wanting to cry again. Her chest ached because his touch reminded her of Daddy's, which she would never feel again. She snorted, blinked and smiled at her uncle.

"See you Friday," he said.

Aunt Celia went outside with Uncle Jimmy and they spoke for a few minutes before he left. Christine hurried to her room to examine her treasure in private.

She also had to write a letter.

Chapter 17

Sam, Cass and Jamie raced down the steps, with Josh tottering behind them. The force of their hugs almost flattened Christine, but she didn't mind. It was great to be with them. Although she felt they'd been apart forever, only two weeks had passed. Josh pulled at her pants and Christine lifted him.

"You're getting heavy," Christine said, kissing his cheek.

"Kwistee!" He squealed.

She was relieved they looked so well. Cass and Jamie seemed bigger than when she'd last seen them. She'd bet they didn't miss their usual diet of food that came out of cans. Christine imagined they would have pined after her and lost weight.

You're reading too many orphan stories, she told herself.

The girls dragged Christine to their dorm, which was empty. The sounds of the children playing outside drifted to them.

"Are you *really* okay?" Christine asked both girls, tugging on their plaits.

They nodded, but didn't smile.

"We miss you," Cass said, "but it not so bad."

"An' we have new friends," Jamie added.

"Our house-mother nice too," Cass said.

Christine started to correct their speech, but guilt kept her silent. Life was so much better for her. Cass and Jamie still didn't understand why they couldn't be together, and Christine had tried explaining how a will worked, but her words hadn't meant much to them. She understood, but hadn't accepted the unfairness of the situation forced on them.

Sighing, Christine told herself things could be worse if they had gone to a home farther away. At least they'd be together once each week. Though Christine had begged to come earlier, Auntie said they needed time to settle. She'd spoken with their housemothers and said they were okay, but that hadn't reassured Christine.

Auntie spent time with the four of them and discussed their progress with their house-mothers. Half way into the visit, Auntie remembered the ripe bananas and oranges she brought with them and asked Christine to get them from the car.

When it was time to leave, Christine's heart dropped to her belly, and it took every scrap of energy to move toward the Suzuki. It hurt all over again to leave her family.

Josh refused to let her go and Auntie B picked him up to stop him from following Christine down the front steps. Sam said he was going back to his dorm and pretended he didn't want to cry, while Cass and Jamie sat on the ledge, wiping their eyes.

"Remember, I'm coming back next week," Christine said, hugging them. That made them cry harder.

Auntie B kept hold of Josh, while Cass and Jamie sniffled. Josh's screams forced tears to Christine's eyes and she wished again that she hadn't made the wish that caused Daddy to die.

On the drive home, Christine gazed out the window. It was just as well she had to tidy up the letter to Roma before sealing it in an envelope. That would take her mind off things. She wanted the letter to be neat and say everything she intended. She'd read it again when she got back to Auntie's house—home, she corrected herself.

Auntie glanced sideways at her. "D'you think you're up to making a trip to see Ellie at the asylum?"

Christine was sure she heard wrong, so she turned to look at Auntie. "Sorry. I didn't hear what you said."

When Auntie repeated her words, the day turned dark and the bottom dropped out of Christine's world. She didn't want to see Ma'am. Not today. Not tomorrow. Not ever.

Chapter 18

Christine chewed the top of her pen while reading what she'd written. At the thought of a possible visit to the asylum, her brow wrinkled and her tummy hurt. She pressed both hands to her stomach and decided to set worrying aside to deal with the letter in front of her. If she was lucky, she wouldn't have to see Ma'am.

July 20,

Dear Mrs. Douglas:

I hope you and your family are well. My name is Christine Simms and I am eleven years old. I like reading and I want to be a teacher like my Aunt Celia and you.

As you know, my father Maxwell Simms passed away this month. After he died, Aunt Celia told me about you. I asked to meet your brother and he came to visit me. He told me all about you and I decided to write this letter. I hope you don't mind.

I also wanted to tell you I'm doing okay. It was great to find out that I have a real mother.

It would be really nice to meet you someday.

Yours truly,

Christine wondered how to sign the letter. Should she write 'your daughter Christine' or just sign her first name? After thinking about it for a bit, she decided on her full name.

She lay across the double bed she now considered her own, propped her head on one arm, thinking over all she'd said in the letter.

She longed to write more, but figured she shouldn't say everything in the first letter. While she hoped her mother would be glad to hear from her, it was probably best not to get too hopeful. After all, Roma Wint, now Douglas, *had* abandoned her.

What would it be like to meet her mother? Behind her eyelids, she saw herself being hugged by a loving woman, who looked like the one in the picture Uncle Jimmy had given her. Crossing her fingers, Christine hoped everything would go the way she dreamed.

After another few minutes of daydreaming, Christine found Aunt Celia in the kitchen and asked her to okay the letter. She wiped her hands on a towel and took the notepaper from Christine, her gaze sweeping back and forth as she read.

"It sounds fine to me," she said, "You seem to have covered everything."

"Thanks, Auntie," Christine said, taking back the sheet of paper.

She returned to her room, where she slid the letter into an envelope, licked and sealed it.

True to his word, Jimmy Wint came back on Friday. He didn't stay long and just before he left, he hugged Christine. His arms were gentle and his clothes smelled of something nice that tickled her nostrils. Christine hugged him, careful not to hold him too tight in case he thought she was mental.

Her eyes went a bit weepy because he was the only link between herself and her mother, and that connection would disappear when he left. She told herself not to worry. He did say he'd come back in a few months. Maybe, he'd bring news of her mother. A letter in return would be awesome.

She hugged herself, watching Uncle Jimmy drive away. For the next few days, she was certain the only thing on her mind would be her mother and whether she'd answer the letter.

A week passed before Aunt Celia raised the matter of Christine seeing Ma'am again. On Saturday, after their visit to Sam, Cass, Jamie and Josh, they sat on the verandah outside the pastry shop in the shade of a huge pink and white striped umbrella. Auntie had suggested stopping to buy ice cream to take home and had treated herself and Christine to a cone first.

Memories of past visits to Arnie's Eatery with her father brought a smile to Christine's face.

Although the afternoon was hot, the constant breeze made being outdoor bearable. Auntie crunched at the last bit of the waffle cone, while Christine licked her ice cream, enjoying the flavor of Pistachio nuts.

Auntie took a packet of moist napkins from her bag and wiped her hands and mouth. She handed one to Christine and dropped the container on the table. "Have you thought any more about seeing Ellie?" she asked.

Christine stopped in the middle of wiping her lips. She rested her hand on the tabletop and swallowed past the roadblock in her throat. If she didn't know differently, she'd think a clump of the cone had lodged there.

"Do I have to?" she whispered.

"She's asking for you."

"Why? She used to say she couldn't bear to look at me."

The ice cream was beginning to melt, so Auntie took the cone from Christine and handed her the napkin they got with the ice cream.

"I don't want to go," Christine said, ripping the napkin.

"I know, but she wants to tell you something."

Auntie ran her palm up and down Christine's arm. "I'll be there with you the whole time."

She took Christine's chin in her hand and looked her in the eyes. "I won't leave you alone with her. I promise."

The reassurance did not improve Christine's mood.

"Will I have to go again, if I visit this time?" Christine asked, pressing a hand to her tummy.

"No. I won't make you visit Ellie unless it's absolutely necessary."

Christine's stomach gurgled as though she had taken the 'wash out' they used to get at the end of summer. Ma'am always said the nasty tasting herbal tea cleaned out their insides. Christine sighed and hoped she wouldn't have an accident. "When do we have to go?"

"Let's do it later today and forget about it."

Christine nodded and didn't complain when Auntie threw the cone in the garbage bin. She wouldn't have enjoyed the rest of the ice cream anyway.

Auntie scooped up the bits of napkin and dumped them.

Christine stared at the patterns on the tabletop, wishing it was evening and the worst part of the day already past. Auntie squeezed her hand and called her name several times before she stood.

"It won't be that bad and it'll be over before you know it, okay?"

"Sure," Christine mumbled, certain that bad didn't begin to describe what seeing Ma'am would be like.

Auntie looked sideway at her and held her hand tight as they crossed the street and got into the car. Christine closed her eyes for a second.

"Calm down," she whispered.

Her heart didn't listen. It pumped madly and her stomach hurt as if a giant hand had grabbed it and squeezed hard. She'd felt the same way each time Ma'am was about to give her a beating.

Chapter 19

Christine sat as still as a figurine in the plastic chair at the foot of Ma'am's bed. Auntie sat next to her, with her handbag on her lap.

The room had a narrow bed, a bedside table and a closet. Christine figured it suited Ma'am fine since she'd never done much more than lie down and talk about how bad her head hurt.

"Hello, Christine. Celia."

"Hello, Ma'am," Christine said, trying not to squirm in the seat. Auntie also told Ma'am howdy.

"You takin' care of your brothers and sisters?"

Christine's eyes snapped to Auntie's face. She cleared her throat and gripped her handbag. "They don't live in the same place, remember?"

Christine studied Ma'am while the wheels in her mind turned non-stop. Something was different about Ma'am. She was calmer than usual. Her body sat across from Christine, but it seemed she was not inside her skin. She acted just as she did after smoking those awful-smelling cigarettes she said settled her nerves.

She's taking medicine. That must be it.

Ma'am cut into her thoughts. "What you mean?"

"The last time I was here, I told you Christine now lives with me," Auntie said.

Christine pulled her head back to look at Auntie. She didn't know they'd had any contact, but supposed that must have been how Auntie knew Ma'am wanted her to visit.

Ma'am responded with a question. "How them doin'?"

"Fine," Celia said, "we saw them earlier today."

"You think I could see..?" Ma'am stopped, as if she had forgotten what she was going to say. Auntie got up and went to stand in the open doorway, facing the corridor.

She spoke to someone, but Christine couldn't make out their words. She also couldn't see the person properly, but saw a pair of white pant legs and shoes of the same colour.

From under her lashes, Christine kept an eye on Ma'am, who stared at her with an expression Christine couldn't read. Her voice sounded rusty when she spoke. "Maxwell's little princess."

Christine started at the familiar words, but this time, they didn't carry the usual meanness Ma'am put into them and her expression didn't change.

"How you doin' without him?"

Christine's slid a glance to the doorway, where Auntie stood, and took comfort in the steady hum of her voice. While considering Ma'am's question, heat stirred in Christine's chest and her face went hot. Her fingers tangled with each other as her thoughts tumbled together.

Why would Ma'am care? She'd taken away the person who cared most about Christine in the world. Sam, Cass, Jamie and Josh were in the home because of what she'd done. She had ripped everything familiar apart and forced a whole new life on them.

Christine's pursed her lips and curled her hands into fists. She wanted to say so much, but fear of Ma'am stole her words. She sucked in some air and pasted on the blank face she usually showed Ma'am. "I'm managing."

Ma'am nodded as though she understood.

"But why did you have to kill him?" Christine asked, her voice dropping to a whisper.

Ma'am didn't get a chance to answer since Aunt Celia came back to sit beside Christine. "You okay?" she asked.

Christine nodded, wondering if Ma'am had heard her question.

"Ellie, it's almost the end of visiting hours, so we have to leave you now," Auntie said.

Christine got up fast and mumbled goodbye. She shot through the door, glaring at Ma'am and leaving Auntie.

Doors lined either side of the corridor and Christine wondered about the people who lived behind them, but didn't stop walking until she reached the open area out front.

She leaned against the wall, breathing hard and staring at the tiles. Although she hadn't got an answer to her question, she thanked God the visit was over.

When Auntie walked up to her, Christine stuck her hand in hers and stayed close until they left the building. The next time Christine spoke, they were in the car, heading home. "She's different. Is it the medicine?"

Aunt Celia nodded, not taking her eyes off the road.

"I don't know what was so urgent, because she never said anything important."

"Maybe she wanted to hear directly from you that your brothers and sisters are doing all right. She knows you love them."

Christine closed her eyes and laid her head against the seat, wishing she could wipe her memory clean of that visit.

She woke when the car crunched to a stop in their driveway. Yawning, she rubbed her eyes with the back of her hands and got out of the Suzuki.

"Later, Auntie," she mumbled, hoping she'd be able to continue her nap. That's if she could sleep, because she still didn't know what Ma'am wanted and hoped she wouldn't send for her again.

Christine sat on the kitchen stool while Auntie prepared ham and cheese sandwiches for supper. She almost believed she'd been doing this for a long time, but accepted it as wishful thinking or a case of déjà vu. Auntie's company made her more comfortable than she'd felt at home. She picked up a bit of hard dough bread crust and chewed one end.

"Didn't Ma'am know about me before she married Daddy?"

Auntie smiled and put down the knife. "It's question time again, eh?"

Christine nodded.

Leaning against the countertop, Aunt Celia spoke. "To answer your question, yes and no. When Max met your mother, he didn't tell her about you up front. That came later."

"Daddy must have asked her to take care of me, right?"

"Yes, he did. We talked about it. Max felt both of you were a package deal. There couldn't be one without the other, so Ellie knew she would have to raise you as her child."

"I still don't know why she hates me," Christine mumbled. "I'd really like to find out."

"I can't say Ellie hates you, but if I were to make a guess, I'd say she probably resented the relationship between your dad and Roma. My brother was honest. He wasn't ready for another relationship when Ellie came along and I know he told her so, but Ellie could be a steamroller when she put her mind to it."

Auntie moved to a cupboard and came back with cling wrap and a platter for the sandwiches. She laid the tray on the counter, and Christine waited.

"Although Ellie agreed to take care of you, I think it hurt her when Max continued to pine after Roma, even after it was clear she wasn't coming back. Max wasn't perfect, but he deserved better. You both did."

"That's true," Christine said, nodding.

"You look angry," Auntie said.

"I get that way when I remember how Ma'am treated me." Christine's brow crumpled. "So you think Daddy loved my moth—" She brushed at a sprinkling of bread crumbs and changed what she'd been about to say. "Roma more than he loved Ellie?"

"I know he did. Roma and he had something really special. His relationship with Ellie was different."

"Why d'you think they got married?" Christine asked.

"Max wanted stability for both of you. He thought he found that in Ellie."

She muttered, and Christine only heard half of what she said. "What?"

"Sorry," Auntie said, "I was talking to myself. You know what they say about your mental state if you start doing that."

Christine looked at the counter so Auntie wouldn't see into her eyes. If she did, she'd know Christine had not only heard some of what she said, but was working it out in her head. Christine wasn't sure what *sacrificing his happiness* meant, but could make a good guess.

"Hmm. I wonder why they stayed together." Christine sat with her cheek resting in her hand. "Things were always crazy at our house and I don't remember it ever being better. All they did was argue every day. Well, Ma'am did the quarrelling and Daddy listened."

"It's hard to leave your home or end a marriage when there are children to consider," Celia said, touching Christine's cheek. "Even if Max hadn't died, he never would have walked away. He loved you all too much. As bad as things were, he still did a great job raising his kids."

A smile broke over Christine's face and she nodded. "That's true too."

Aunt Celia moved the sandwiches from the cutting board to the platter and then covered them with cling wrap. She shook her head, smiled and then smoothed the edges of the plastic under the serving plate.

"What is it, Auntie?"

"Sometimes, I forget you're only eleven. As my mother used to say, you have an old soul."

"Daddy told me that too."

Christine returned the cling wrap to the cupboard, her mind occupied with Auntie's words. If Roma had been strong enough to go against what her parents wanted and had stayed with Daddy, Ma'am wouldn't have ended up married to him and he wouldn't be dead.

More than ever, Christine was determined to meet the woman who had changed their lives. She had a lot of explaining to do.

Chapter 20

Celia closed her bedroom door and sat at the dressing table. She dropped a handful of letters on the polished wood, willing her heart to slow its rapid beat. Carefully, she slit the sole airmail envelope and unfolded the letter she'd left for last.

August 10,

Dear Celia,

It's been a long time. I was shocked to hear of Maxwell's death. Please accept my condolence on his passing.

I received Christine's letter and by the sound of it, she is a fine young woman. Many things have changed since I left the island. I'm married and my husband doesn't know about Christine, so you will appreciate what a big surprise her letter has been and how hard it is for me to deal with.

Although she's wants to meet me, I'm not prepared for that now. There are many things I need to sort out before I can take such a big step. Maybe I'll feel differently as time goes by.

I had planned to come home at the end of the year for a family reunion, so who knows, maybe we'll meet then.

Many thanks for what you're doing for Christine. Jimmy tells me she now lives with you. Over the years, I've never forgotten the kindness you showed me during the time Maxwell and I were together.

As it relates to Christine, I've been sadly lacking, and despite what you might feel, I do think about her. I hope at some point I can do what needs to be done for my child. For now, I'm enclosing a small token of my appreciation.

Yours,
Roma

Celia slipped the hundred Canadian dollars back in the envelope and read the letter again. It confirmed what she'd suspected Roma's answer to Christine's letter would be. However, she had responded earlier than Celia expected.

Roma *would* have difficulty explaining her sudden acquisition of an eleven-year-old daughter, but Celia was outraged that after ignoring Christine's existence for so long, her mother would send a note and a hundred dollars, hoping to fix the ills she had caused by leaving.

Christine's unfolding horror stories of her experiences with Ellie were nothing a child should have endured.

Celia pressed both hand over her eyes and pulled back her shoulders although she felt like bawling. What possible explanation could she give Christine for Roma not replying directly to her? Celia stared at the swirls in the wood, working out what to say.

After a while, she got up and went to find Christine.

She went across the living room to the other side of the house and knocked on the bedroom door. When Christine chirped for her to 'come in', Celia entered.

Over time, Christine was stamping her character on the room. She had slipped a headshot of Max under the wood framing the mirror. Another photo of the entire family sat on top of the dressing table. Christine had also laid out various projects from her art and craft classes on the dresser.

Celia smiled when she thought about the changes in the household. Michael still found Christine reserved and Claude was getting used to the cousin he had only seen once or twice before. In Celia's opinion, the family had passed the first few hurdles satisfactorily.

Christine would be all right.

She rolled over and sat up, then placed a tasselled bookmarker inside the novel she was reading and closed it. Celia looked around the room again before sitting on the wicker chair next to the bed.

"I wanted to talk to you about school before I did anything."

"Okay," Christine said, laying the book beside her.

"D'you want to continue at your old school, which is still close enough or would you like to attend school here in Hoopersville?"

"I'd prefer to go to school here," Christine said. "It would be like starting over."

"All right. I'll arrange a transfer. You know you'll be in the same school with me, right?"

Christine nodded. "That's not a big deal. In fact, I'd like that."

When she grinned, Celia sat beside her on the bed and took one of Christine's hands in hers.

"I've heard from your mother," she said gently.

"Really? What did she say? Can I see the letter? Is she coming to visit me?" Christine's eyes lit up and with each question, she bounced on the mattress. Celia held up one arm to stop the torrent of questions and with the other, tightened her hold on Christine's hand.

"She got your letter and wrote back to say she's proud of you."

Christine closed her eyes as though praying, her expression blissful. Celia shifted and shook their clasped hands until Christine's eyes opened.

"She says she may come home in December."

Christine sprang off the bed and danced around the room, humming to a lively tune and beaming as she went.

Celia waved Christine back to her side. It was wonderful to see Christine behaving like a carefree child, but it pained Celia to have to give her news that would mar her happiness. "Come sit with me for a moment."

Christine flopped on the bed and hugged Celia around the waist. She's such an affectionate little thing, Celia thought, forcing herself to pay attention when Christine started speaking.

"I'm so happy. The last time I was this happy..." Whatever she remembered made her voice trail off and she hunched, but straightened after a moment and looked at Celia, her gaze suspicious.

"I know there's something more." Christine withdrew her hand. "What else did she say?"

"Well, if she comes in December, you'll probably meet her then," Celia said. "She sent money for you, so we can get you some things on our next shopping trip."

"That's nice," Christine said, clearly unimpressed.

She folded her arms over her flat chest and gazed at Celia. "Auntie, why didn't she answer *my* letter?"

"Well..."

"If she's *so* proud of me, why couldn't she write and tell me so herself?"

Christine lowered her head until her gaze found the mat by the side of the bed.

Feeling like a hypocrite, Celia resorted to damage control. "Christine, we have to be fair. This isn't as easy for her as you think. It must have been a shock to hear from you for the first time since..."

"Since she forgot that I exist?"

"I was going to say, since she left the island." Celia licked her lips and chose her words with care. "She has a far different life and..."

"Other children," Christine mumbled, wriggling her bare toes on the mat's fringe.

Celia didn't acknowledge Christine's sullen words. Instead, she hugged her. "Sweet Pea, this is hard to digest, but I'm going to ask you to be patient with her."

Christine smiled, as she did every time Celia called her by that name. She blinked a few times before asking, "D'you think I'm ever going to meet her?"

Celia reached for the crucifix, but let her hand fall to her lap without making contact. "I think so. She's interested in meeting you, but it will take her a while to get used to the idea."

"You think if I wrote her again that would make her decide quicker?"

"No, hon, I don't think that's such a good idea."

Christine's face settled into stubborn lines and her eyes filled again. "She's just a big old coward."

"Christine, you're not being fair."

"I shoulda known better anyway. She never business when she lef', so why she woulda business now?"

Celia pressed a hand to her chest. This was the first time she'd heard Christine speak Patois, but there was no point in taking her to task over it. She was entitled. Hiding her disquiet, Celia searched for a suitable explanation. "It's not that she doesn't care, it's just that..."

Christine raised an eyebrow, which defied any explanation Celia could give.

Her breath seeped out in a defeated sigh. She scratched her ear and couldn't find the words to lie to Christine. Celia had never condoned any form of deceit and didn't plan to start practicing now.

"You know what?" Christine grabbed the book she'd put on the bed and threw it aside. "I don't care anymore. I hate her too. I hate her just as much as Ma'am! Di two of dem can jus'..."

Christine paused as she searched for suitable words. "Go jump off a high building, for all I care. The only person who ever loved me anyway was Daddy."

That said, Christine flung herself across the bed, sobbing. Celia had no idea what to say to lessen her pain. Through the tears scorching her own eyes, Celia said, "I'll talk to you in a while."

She left the room, wishing she'd kept her trap shut and that she could go back in time to when Christine knew nothing about her mother.

Chapter 21

When her tears stopped, Christine slipped into the bathroom and washed her face. In front of the mirror, she eyed her reflection. Most times, she could find a reason to laugh. This time, she couldn't work up a tiny smile.

She went back to her room, straightened the sheet on the bed and continued reading. The words wouldn't stick and she got annoyed because she kept remembering Ma'am. She stuck a finger inside the book to mark the page and lay on her side, staring at the patterns on the sheet.

A spark of an idea came to life and the more Christine thought, the more she liked it.

She'd write to her mother again. She had a few words to say that couldn't wait until her iffy trip in December. At the rate things were going, years might pass before they met. She'd have to deal with this herself, which was fine. She'd been taking care of business her whole life. This would be no different.

Christine got out her notepad. She pushed aside bottles of body mist and lotion on the dressing table, sized herself up in the mirror, and started writing.

August 24,

Dear Mrs. Douglas,
Aunt Celia told me you wrote to her. Thanks very much for the money.
I was happy to know you wrote a letter, but I wonder why you didn't reply to the one I sent. I was so looking forward to hearing from you.

Aunt Celia said you might be coming in December. I hope to meet you, but I'd be even happier if you answered me, so I'll know you really exist.

My letter must have been a surprise, since you probably forgot me. I understand why you couldn't take care for me, since my aunt explained everything. Daddy did his best, but now he's gone, so it would be nice if you wrote to me sometime.

Christine

She folded the letter and slipped it into the book. She picked up her pen, tore a half leaf from an exercise book and then went from room to room, looking for Auntie. When she reached the kitchen without finding her, Christine stood in front of the double windows facing the backyard.

Aunt Celia sat in her favourite spot under the Mango tree, a book in her lap and sipping from a tall glass of lemonade. Since the weather was hot, Christine figured Auntie would be out there for a while. She turned to leave the kitchen and jumped when Uncle Michael's hand landed on her shoulder.

Uncle's eyebrows scrunched together and he squinted behind wire-rimmed glasses. "You all right Christine?"

"Yes, Sir," she said, hoping he couldn't see she was breathing faster than normal.

"Where's Celia?"

Christine pointed toward the backyard.

"Thanks." He opened the back door and walked across the grass.

Crushing the paper in her fist, Christine looked out the window again. Uncle Michael now sat beside Auntie on a plastic patio chair, his hairy legs stretched out. After they talked for a bit, Uncle took off his glasses, lay back and closed his eyes.

Christine made a second attempt to leave the kitchen and rolled her eyes when Claude came into the room.

"Hey, Christine." He hiked his glasses up on his nose and headed for the fridge.

"Hi, yourself." Christine shook her head, predicting what Claude was going to do, since he was forever hungry. She stuck around until he reached for the loaf of bread and then hurried away, pen and paper in hand.

She snuck into Aunt Celia's room, closing the door gently. Standing still for a moment, she scanned the huge bed in the middle of the room and the padded sheet that matched the cream curtains.

Although nobody could hear her, Christine tiptoed to the dressing table and took up a stack of envelopes. Most of them were bills. She replaced the pile. Where to look next?

She opened one of the top drawers. Nothing inside but brushes, combs and hair clips. Eyeing the door, she slid the drawer shut and wished her heart would stop fluttering.

Inside the other drawer lay two envelopes, one baby pink and the other with airmail colours. Christine's hands shook as she lifted them and turned over the airmail envelope. There on the left corner, was a small label. She brought it closer to her eyes. A yellow rose was printed beside her mother's name and address.

Ignoring her galloping heart and moving faster than she ever had before, Christine scribbled the information on the bit of paper and put it in her skirt.

She longed to find out what was in the letter and her hand crept out, but she was too nervous. She looked across the room again. If she stayed much longer, someone might catch her. She tore off a stamp from a sheet inside the drawer and stuck it in her pocket, hoping Auntie wouldn't miss it. After replacing both envelopes, Christine crossed to the door.

She raised her hand to open it but the handle turned and the door swung inward. She hopped back to avoid being hit and dropped the pen, which rolled across the floor. Heat flooded her face and she picked up the pen, trying not to look as guilty as she felt. As she straightened, she recognized Uncle Michael's hairy legs and coconut knees. His eyebrows questioned her. "Christine, what are you doing? You needed something?"

"Uh, yes." Christine did a slow march from one leg to the other.

"I came to find a pen," she said, holding it up.

"Okay, fine."

Christine ignored his puzzled stare and shuffled sideways past him. Uncle muttered and went farther into the room.

She raced across the living room to the other end of the house, gripping the material around her pocket. In her room, she leaned against the closed door, breathing hard. "That was close."

If she was lucky, Uncle Michael might believe that whopper. She hated lying, but this time it was for a good reason.

She got the letter out of the book, wrote on the envelope and sealed it. Her task complete, she lay down, drained of energy. All that subterfuge wore a body out.

"Subterfuge," she whispered.

Another new word added to her vocabulary. She'd seen it in one of the books she'd read last week.

Daddy would be proud to know she was keeping up with her reading and widening her vocabulary. He always said if she continued to do well in school, she'd grow up to be someone special.

If her mother had thought any such thing she wouldn't have gone off and left her. Christine's gaze landed on the dresser where the envelope rested under the doily.

All she had to do now was mail the letter and wait to see if her mother would respond.

Chapter 22

The next eight weeks passed in a blur as Christine settled into school. Among her special friends was Jacqueline Sawyers, who lived on the same block and was in her class. Jackie invited Christine to her house several times and as they grew closer, Auntie allowed Jackie to come over so they could do homework and study together.

They sat in Christine's bedroom giggling after Claude left the room.

"He's lost in love," Christine declared in a throaty voice, one hand spread on her chest.

Depending on the day of the week and his mood, Claude either loved or hated Jackie. Today, he was in love and had brought her lemonade. He was functioning well enough to remember to also bring a glass for Christine. The girls figured he'd be back in a few minutes with a different reason for visiting.

"Boys!" Jackie rolled her almond-shaped eyes. Her ponytail bobbed as she laughed.

"Aw, give him a chance." Christine poked Jackie with her elbow and gave in to a fresh attack of giggles. Another knock came at the door and they looked at each other, thinking Claude had returned with another gift.

"Come in," Christine yelled.

Aunt Celia's head and shoulders appeared around the door. "I'm just checking on you guys. You're laughing so hard, you can't be getting much work done."

"We'll get right back to work," Christine said.

"Make sure you do. It will be dark soon and Jackie'll have to head home," Aunt Celia said and pulled the door shut.

Between sips of lemonade, they completed their homework and then quizzed each other at spelling, which lasted another fifteen minutes.

While Jackie got her books together, she whispered to Christine. "Any word yet?"

"No, and it's been more than two months." Christine scratched at a bubblegum sticker she had pasted inside her book.

"Maybe she took a while to write back," Jackie said. "Plus, you know how slow they say the mail is in Jamaica."

"I dunno." Christine shook her head slowly from side to side. "It's been more than enough time now."

"Wait a little longer and see what happens," Jackie said.

"There's nothing else I can do anyway," Christine said and got up to clear the desk.

"See you tomorrow!" Jackie yelled as her mother opened the grille to let her inside.

Aunt Celia and Christine waved goodbye and turned back down the block toward their house. Christine stifled a yawn, wanting to sleep although it was only a few minutes past seven.

Her hand swung with Auntie's as they strolled down the sidewalk. Christine's head dipped when she remembered that Daddy used to hold her hand like this. Pinpricks spread in her eyes, but she sucked in some air and tried not to think about Daddy.

Christine pictured her mother's face and wondered who her sons resembled, but her thoughts kept going back to Daddy, alone in a box in the cemetery.

Auntie squeezed her hand and Christine looked up at her.

"You girls have really taken to each other," Auntie said "and Claude seems to like her too."

"Yeah, Jackie's all right. She's the first friend I made at school. She came up to me that first day and just started talking."

"If you ask me, she hasn't stopped since." Auntie teased Christine, smiling. "The two of you chat a lot when you're supposed to be doing homework."

"We do talk a whole heap," Christine admitted, "but it's because we like the same things: reading, ice cream, art and craft. You know, girl stuff."

"Just as long as you're getting your work done, I'm happy." Auntie loosed Christine's hand to open their gate. In the living room, she stopped Christine with a touch on the shoulder. "Your teacher tells me you're doing well. Max would be pleased."

Christine nodded and blinked a few times when the pinpricks started up in her eyes again. "I wish…"

She stopped, but Auntie didn't ask what she wanted to say. Christine dragged her feet toward her room, unable to share what was on her mind.

"Christine?"

Auntie stood in the same position, motioning to her.

Christine returned to Auntie, her mouth turned down at the corners. Auntie pulled her into a hug, speaking above her head. "Things may seem dark sometimes, but they do get better."

"I just wish my mother would respond to my letter," Christine said, sighing.

"In a way, she did," Auntie said. "It might not have been the response you hoped for, but at least she contacted us and that's something, isn't it?"

Christine took a small step back and spoke in a mournful voice, "But she must have got my *other* letter by now."

Auntie's wide eyes and loud gasp made Christine clap a hand over her mouth. She flashed a glance at Auntie, wishing she could take back her words.

Auntie squeezed Christine's shoulders way too tight. "What other letter?"

"I-I sort of wrote to her again," Christine said, eyes fixed on the squiggly patterns in the tiles.

"You did what?" Auntie raised Christine's head by lifting her chin. "Where did you get her address?"

"From your room," Christine whispered. "In your drawer."

"I can't believe you did that. You know you're not supposed to search other people's things, right?"

Christine nodded, but couldn't look at Auntie. She'd never done anything like that before, but thought she'd do it again, if necessary.

"I know you're anxious to meet your mother, but that's no reason to do what you did."

Although she felt awful inside, Christine was relieved Auntie knew what she'd done. Her wait would be less lonesome.

Auntie stepped back and folded her arms. "When did you do it?"

Christine mumbled to the floor, not daring to face Auntie. When she finished explaining, Auntie sighed and hugged her again. Speaking into her hair, she said, "You do know that I'm going to have to punish you, don't you?"

Christine nodded and although unsure how she'd be punished, she wasn't afraid. Auntie would never hit her like Ma'am had done.

Christine raised her head and met Auntie's gaze. "I don't want to cause any trouble. I just want…" She hesitated, not sure she should admit what she was thinking. "I just want her to love me."

"Christine, there are people who love you. *I* love you. I haven't told you, but I do." Auntie cupped Christine's cheeks. "In the short time we've been together, you've become the daughter I never had. Whether Roma responds to you or not, you'll still be you and you're special. I want you to remember that."

Christine closed her eyes and enjoyed the stroking of Auntie's thumbs across her brow. She couldn't remember Ma'am touching her that way.

"Go read something to relax your brain and get some rest, Sweet Pea. I'll see you tomorrow," Auntie said, kissing Christine's forehead.

"G'nite, Auntie." Christine went down the passage, hugging herself. This was the first time anybody but Daddy had kissed her. She'd had a couple of wonderful 'firsts' today.

"And by the way," Auntie Celia called, "For your little adventure, there will be no television for the next two weeks."

Christine nodded and hid a smile. Having no television wasn't so bad, considering what she'd done. She wouldn't miss it anyway.

In bed, she replayed the conversation she'd had with Auntie and was thankful she hadn't been too mad. Things could have been much worse.

It was nice to be loved, but the fact still remained, she needed a real mother, like every other girl she knew. She had written two times with nothing to show for it, but there had to be a way to make her mother pay attention. Maybe Uncle Jimmy could help, but she didn't know how to reach him, and she couldn't ask Auntie for help.

After all of that effort, it would have been good to know her mother was interested in her, but that didn't seem to be the case.

Her eyelids dipped. Tomorrow was another day. Somehow, she'd find a way to make her mother wake up and admit her child existed.

Chapter 23

Octorber slipped by without a word from Roma, while Celia grew even closer to Christine. She spoke of Roma less often, but Celia was sure Christine still hoped she'd meet her mother. Celia caught her countless times wearing a dreamy smile while she stared at Roma's photograph.

The way Christine continued to fantasize and pine after Roma—who had disappointed them both—cut Celia deep. But what to do? She didn't want to say anything to make Christine admit what was obvious; Roma had no clue what to do about Christine's advances.

At the end of November, Jimmy Wint returned to the island and asked to see Christine. Celia hesitated to say yes because Christine had settled into a comfortable routine.

He called ahead, saying he had news and wouldn't budge when Celia tried to get information out of him. He only said he preferred to speak to her in person. She agreed to meet him at the coffee shop one afternoon while Christine was at Drama club.

Celia arrived before Jimmy and sat under an umbrella enjoying the breeze until he drove up and approached her table.

Jimmy took a seat across from her, looking the same as the last time he'd visited, except that he had lines on his forehead she hadn't noticed before. He kept both hands busy, folding and unfolding a bit of paper.

"Would you like a drink?" she asked.

"No, I'm fine. Thanks."

She took a sip of Lime Squash, still enjoying the wind's gentle caress. "How come you're back so soon? I didn't expect to see you before next month."

"Well, since we're having this family reunion, I came back early to help make arrangements."

"I see," Celia said.

Jimmy's gaze shifted to hers when she put down the glass.

"So what's up?"

"Roma got another letter from Christine," he said, meeting her eyes.

"She wrote without my consent or knowledge."

"Roma was upset at first. She felt she was being forced into a corner, but now realizes Christine is just anxious to meet her."

Celia wiped her hands on a napkin, unsure of what was coming next. "So what news d'you have?"

"Roma is coming for the reunion next month, but she's still uncertain how to handle the situation with Christine."

Celia barely stopped herself from rolling her eyes. Although she'd told Christine to stop doing it, Celia had picked up the habit. She chose her words so as not to offend. "I understand how complicated this whole business is, but after three months, I thought she'd have made up her mind what to do."

Jimmy looked away, rubbing his chin. "She still hasn't told her husband about this—Christine yet."

"I know she can't spring this on him, but wouldn't it be easier to just get it over with, if she plans to do it at all?"

"She wants to meet Christine," Jimmy said, drumming his fingers on the tabletop. "But…"

Celia couldn't say how she knew what Jimmy was going to say, but finished his sentence. "She'd prefer if nobody knows about it."

Jimmy looked at her, his mouth half-open. "How did you guess?"

"It wasn't hard to figure out, considering her silence."

Jimmy avoided her eyes and continued tapping a beat on the table's surface.

"The only good thing is that Christine is so eager to meet Roma she won't care too much if she doesn't meet anyone else in your family. At least, for now."

"Oh, I do want her to meet my kids—her cousins," Jimmy cut in, sounding flustered.

"So they'll be coming too?"

"Actually, they live here."

"Oh? I thought your family lived in Canada?"

Jimmy shifted, but didn't answer. Celia took another sip of her drink and told herself to stop asking questions. From his reaction, it was clear she had intruded on Jimmy's privacy.

They parted ways after agreeing that he'd visit Christine on Saturday afternoon.

Celia finished her drink, praying Christine wouldn't have to face any more heartbreak.

Chapter 24

Christine tried not to grab the boxed set of books Uncle Jimmy handed her when he stepped on the verandah.

"These are from your mother," he said.

Auntie invited him to sit, while Christine examined her gift. She took out the book in front, flipped it open and read the handwritten note.

"How did she know?" She beamed. "This is just what I wanted to read next. We saw the movie on our book club trip and I couldn't wait to read the books."

"I'll let her know you like them," Uncle Jimmy said. "Of course, you could tell her when she comes to the island next month."

"Really?" Christine breathed out and struggled to suck in another breath, carried away the excitement bubbling in her chest. "Cool. I can't wait!"

She wanted to dance around the verandah, but hung on to Auntie's arm instead. "Did you hear that? My mother is coming to Jamaica!"

Aunt Celia returned her grin. "Yes, I heard."

Christine spun through another book before squeezing it to her body. Her eyes closed and her lids fluttered at the vision behind them. The width of her smile hurt her cheeks. Her lashes lifted and she met her uncle's gaze. "What date is she coming?"

"I'm not sure, somewhere around the middle of the month."

"Will I meet my brothers?"

"I-I'm not sure."

Christine's smile faded.

"But I want you to meet my kids," he added, as if his words could wipe away Christine's disappointment. "Your cousins."

She looked at Auntie, who gave her an encouraging smile, but it didn't fool Christine. Auntie was just as concerned. She twisted her wedding bands, frowned at Uncle Jimmy and pulled her mouth into what Christine recognized as her 'I'm-serious-so-don't-play-with-me' look.

Why was it okay to meet her cousins, but not her brothers? Christine's thoughts threatened to run off in various directions, but she couldn't afford that now. She'd think about the reasons later.

Uncle was waiting for her to speak, and knowing he expected her to be excited, Christine forced a smile. "That would be nice."

"When's a good time to take her?" Jimmy asked.

"How about tomorrow?" Auntie said.

"I'll pick her up at noon."

Christine fought worry that tried to push her excitement aside. It would be her first time out without Auntie.

The breeze rustled the Palm trees in the front yard and while watching them swish back and forth, Christine wondered if Auntie would let her go alone. If she was old enough to take care of her brothers and sisters, she was certainly old enough to go on a visit with her uncle.

Uncle Jimmy got up, touching Christine's shoulder. "I have a few more stops to make, so I have to leave now. I'll see you tomorrow."

"I can't wait," Christine said, grinning at the thought of meeting other members of her family. She followed her uncle into the front yard, waving until he backed onto the road and drove away.

She hoped she'd get along with her cousins and that when she got to meet her mother, she'd like her even a little bit.

On her way up the steps, she hugged herself. Auntie had gone inside, but the books still lay on the chair. Christine picked up the cardboard package and held it tight to her chest, visualizing her mother.

She looked at the picture every day, wondering what Roma Wint was like. Did she have even a tiny portion of her mother's personality? Would Roma see any resemblance to her? Christine doubted it, since she couldn't see where she looked anything like her mother, even if Uncle Jimmy and Auntie had said so.

Still hugging the books, Christine rushed to her room to have another look at the picture.

Chapter 25

C hristine counted the clusters of wild bushes that zipped by as the car covered the miles to Uncle Jimmy's house. When boredom set in, she examined the dial of the silver watch Aunt Celia had bought her. Twenty minutes had passed since she left home.

She took a quick look at her Uncle, who kept his eyes on the road. He'd tuned in to a radio station he liked and was humming to oldies music. Every so often, he asked if she was okay.

Fingers crossed, Christine hoped her cousins would be fun, but reminded herself of the most important thing that was going to happen to her. Ever. In less than two weeks she'd meet her mother for the first time. Nothing else mattered as much.

Christine started paying attention when they turned into a housing estate. The homes stood on individual lots like Auntie's house, only these seemed larger. Many of them looked the same, but a few had been extended sideways or had another floor added.

When they rolled up and stopped in front of a two-story house, the door opened and a woman and two children stood waiting for them on the verandah.

They went up the walkway, and Christine hung back until Uncle Jimmy pulled her to stand beside him. "Christine, meet Patricia and Simeon and their mother, Mona."

Christine and Patricia sized each other up while Uncle Jimmy introduced them. Patricia resembled her father more than she did her mother. The close-cropped hairstyle made Patricia look like a small copy of him.

She wore a loose tee-shirt and shorts, and the tiny hoops in her ears were the only things that told Christine she was a girl. Patricia was thirteen and flat-chested—a late developer, according to the stuff Christine read about puberty in the books Auntie had bought her.

When Uncle Jimmy wasn't looking, Patricia cut her eyes at Christine and didn't shake her hand or wave. Christine let her hand fall to her side, thinking her cousin was either weird or had a problem.

Simeon, Patricia's ten-year-old brother, welcomed Christine and invited her to play a board game. Their mother, said hello and nothing else.

Christine wondered if they had a quarrel before she came, and sent a glance Uncle Jimmy's way. He seemed okay, which made Christine think Patricia and her mother didn't know how to act around new people.

After a mini-tour, Simeon spread a game of Snakes and Ladders on the living room floor. Patricia sat on the nearest sofa, her brows rumpled in a frown. After a while, she edged closer to watch the game.

Uncle Jimmy disappeared, and the children's mother stayed, watching them with her hands propped on her sides. When Christine thought she'd never leave, Aunt Mona went to the kitchen.

Glancing at Patricia, Christine wondered why her presence would upset her cousin, but didn't believe the girl could be jealous of her. Uncle Jimmy was *her* daddy and she was lucky to have one.

They played several rounds before Christine needed to use the bathroom.

"Come, I'll take you," Patricia said.

Christine followed her upstairs trying to work out why Patricia took her up there when they had a bathroom downstairs. Christine had seen it when Simeon dragged her around, showing her everything.

Christine finished her business, washed her hands and opened the door. Patricia stood in front of it, her feet spread apart and her arms folded.

"Excuse me," Christine said, eyebrows raised.

She stepped out, which forced Patricia to move backward.

"Why Daddy bring you here?" she asked.

"He said he wanted me to meet his children."

"If you're our cousin, how come we neva heard of you before?"

"How am I supposed to know? Uncle Jimmy just found—"

"Uncle Jimmy, Uncle Jimmy." Patricia mimicked Christine, hands on her hips.

"What yuh mother name?"

"Ell—Roma."

Patricia snickered. "Yuh don't know who your mother is?"

Christine's nostrils flew open and her eyes narrowed, but she didn't speak.

"I thought Daddy said she lived in Canada?" Patricia asked, dropping her aggressive manner.

"She does," Christine said, still wondering what was going on with Patricia. "I used to live with my father and he died and then—"

"Are you sure?" Patricia said, pinning Christine with hostile eyes.

"Of course, I'm sure," Christine said. "Which child doesn't know their parents?"

Christine pushed aside the thought that she hadn't known one of hers until recently and had a mind to ask Patricia if she'd lost her senses somewhere.

"I was just checking." Patricia grumbled and turned away.

Christine shook her head and rolled her eyes, and on the way downstairs, decided that her cousin was cuckoo. She acted weird like that girl at school, the one who Jackie said needed to have her head sorted out.

If Patricia hadn't lost her marbles, then maybe she was in a bad mood today. That would explain why she continued to act as if Christine had stolen something from her.

After they got tired of the game, they watched an animated movie. Aunt Mona made popcorn and sandwiches, which she served with tall glasses of Guava juice.

Halfway through the second movie, Uncle Jimmy passed them and went into the kitchen. Moments later, a pot slammed on the stovetop; a sound Christine recognized. She pretended not to hear Uncle Jimmy and Aunt Mona's raised voices and ignored the anxious glances exchanged by Patricia and Simeon.

Uncle Jimmy walked by, grumbling something like 'miserable woman.' Christine kept her gaze on the television screen, wishing it was time to go home. Being in this house reminded her too much of her old life.

Christine blew out a relieved breath when Uncle Jimmy said he was ready to take her home, and though Patricia didn't get any friendlier, she did tell Christine she should come again.

Aunt Mona didn't behave any differently from when they arrived. Maybe she was mad because Uncle Jimmy hadn't told her he was bringing home a visitor.

All the same, Ma'am used to make a fuss over everything, so who knew what was going on with Aunt Mona.

When they pulled up at home, Aunt Celia sat on the verandah reading a book. Her quick smile reassured Christine she was happy to see her. Uncle Jimmy talked to Auntie for a few minutes and left soon after, raising a cloud of dust.

Christine trailed Auntie to the kitchen, telling her how the visit had gone. While she shared the details about the house, Auntie washed cups left in the sink. Christine leaned against the counter, still trying to figure out what had happened earlier in the day.

"Uncle Jimmy's family is kind of strange," she said.

"Does that mean you didn't have fun?"

"I did enjoy myself a little, but Patricia, Uncle Jimmy's daughter, questioned me when I went to use the bathroom."

"What did she ask you?"

"She asked about my mother and I told her about Daddy too. Simeon was okay, but their mother wasn't friendly."

She scrunched her brows together. "Maybe Aunt Mona was mad about something that had nothing to do with me."

"You're probably right."

Christine had a thought and pursed her lips to avoid laughing. Then she said, "I'm telling you, Auntie, she looked at me as if biting ants had run loose inside her clothes."

Aunt Celia tried to hide her smile, but Christine caught her before she put on her serious face. "Young lady, you shouldn't say things like that about your elders."

Christine smoothed a hand over her stomach and tried not to burst out laughing. "Yes, Auntie."

Based on what Aunt Mona said to Uncle Jimmy, he was 'keeping a woman with her'. Christine knew what that meant, but was too thirsty to discuss it with Auntie this minute.

She got herself a glass of lemonade, remembering when she lived with the family. She wouldn't have dared to take anything from the fridge without asking.

At the table, she drank the tangy, ice-cold liquid, and her question to do with Aunt Mona's accusation slipped away.

Chapter 26

Celia couldn't make head or tail of Christine's story, but didn't doubt that her niece's observations were correct.

Now what has Jimmy been up to? Celia asked herself during Christine's non-stop chatter.

Why would his wife be unhappy about Christine's visit? Come to think of it, Jimmy never said anything about being married. He just said he had a family, which could mean anything in Jamaica. Maybe he was married and maybe he wasn't.

What he did in his home was none of her business, as long as it didn't affect Christine. Maybe they were making a mountain out of a molehill.

Perhaps Christine had visited in the middle of some kind of family tension and mistakenly thought it was directed at her.

"Auntie, are you listening?" Christine tapped her arm, which brought Celia's mind back into the room.

"Of course, I am."

"Well, what d'you think?" Christine looked expectant.

"I, er, I guess..."

Christine shook her head, giving Celia a long-suffering look.

"I knew you weren't listening! Auntieeee!" She sighed and put a glass in the sink. "I asked if we can get my mother a gift, for when we meet."

"That's fine," Celia said, still occupied with Jimmy's affairs, despite what she'd told herself. Christine was no fool, which meant something might have been going on. She reminded herself that Jimmy's situation was not her concern and handed Christine a Pyrex dish, which she placed on top of the glassware in the dish-drainer.

Christine voiced her next thought in a soft, dreamy voice, which brought Celia back to earth with a painful bump.

"Wouldn't it be nice if I could live with my mother?"

Chapter 27

The days before her mother's arrival on the island were the longest in Christine's life. She filled them by shadowing Auntie and asking questions. D'you think she'll like me? D'you think we'll get along? What are we gonna buy her? What if she doesn't like her present? Will we spend lots of time together?

Christine was grateful for Auntie's patience and loved her more for it. There was no way she could have pestered Ma'am as she'd done with Auntie. Christine played out various scenes in her mind, but she didn't share them with Auntie.

A few days before her mother arrived, Auntie arranged a shopping trip to make sure Christine looked her best for the meeting. They settled on a light-blue, sleeveless dress that flared at the waist. During every spare moment, Christine tried it on and posed in front of the mirror, spinning this way and that.

Auntie helped select Roma's present, a small wicker basket filled with lavender-scented soaps and candles secured under cling-film. Christine kept her offering hidden in a gift bag, complete with a card, which she had written up in her neatest handwriting.

Her mother arrived on the island on December 18th, during the Christmas holidays. Auntie had set her visit with Christine for the following day and asked Uncle Jimmy to bring Roma to their house. Auntie said Christine would be more comfortable in 'familiar surroundings'.

Christine didn't feel that was necessary, but gave in to Auntie who couldn't seem to stop fussing and said if anything went wrong, Christine would feel better at home.

Auntie worried too much, Christine told herself. Nothing could go wrong on what was going to be a perfect day.

On the morning of the visit, Christine woke at the first hint of daylight. Last night, she'd gone to sleep when she was so tired she couldn't see and her eyelids wouldn't stay open any longer.

She cocked her head, but the house was silent. She tried reading until everybody else got up, but that didn't work, so she showered and got back in bed to fantasize until breakfast time.

Her dream world did not release her fast enough to hear the knock on her door. It opened and Auntie peeked at her. "G'morning, Christine. Today's the day."

"Uh-huh." Christine said around a jaw-breaking smile. "What time is it?"

"Seven-thirty."

"That's all?" Christine rolled her eyes around their sockets, being more dramatic than usual.

"Better relax, Sweet Pea. One o' clock is hours away," Auntie said, smiling.

"Gosh, this will be the loooongest day ever."

"How about helping me make breakfast? That will keep you busy for a little while."

Christine got out of bed, eager to occupy her mind with something other than dreams starring her mother.

After they ate, Auntie prepared to go grocery shopping. They usually went early on Saturday mornings, before the crowds filled the supermarket.

In between racing to put items in the trolley, Christine cast non-stop glances at her watch. The hour hand circled at a sluggish pace, which made Christine think it had stopped working.

When they stood at the cash register, Christine looked hard at the watch and then put it to her ear. She tapped it to make sure it was keeping the right time. After she let her hand rest at her side, Christine caught Auntie smiling.

Christine hurried to the car, pleading silently for the baggage boy to hurry and move their bags from the cart to the trunk. Then, Auntie took ages to tip him, start the car and pull out of the parking lot.

By the time they rolled up in their driveway, Christine's right ankle ached from pressing her imaginary gas pedal. It was 12:15, enough time to put away the groceries and get dressed for the most important meeting of her life.

Chapter 28

Roma Wint-Douglas wore a pink suit, made from a crinkly material. Nobody had ever looked better, Christine thought. Her perfume was wonderful.

Christine sniffed the air, enjoying the delicate scent of roses. Being around Auntie's garden helped her recognize the scent. Her mother wore glasses with brown, rectangular frames and a deep-red lip-stick. To Christine, she was beautiful.

Now that she thought about it, Christine was glad Auntie had arranged the meeting in their home. She wouldn't have to go anywhere to dream about the lovely woman in front of her and go over every word they exchanged. Nobody would disturb them, because Uncle Michael and Claude had gone shopping for tools at the hardware.

"As if he needs any more," Auntie had said earlier. "That man will use any excuse to buy more stuff he doesn't need."

Christine had laughed and reminded Auntie that Uncle Michael said the same thing about the books she bought every other week.

They stood in the middle of the living room and Auntie pulled Christine forward. She came out of her dream world when Auntie spoke, sounding as though she was standing at the far end of a tunnel. Christine didn't catch her words, but put out her hand. Roma's grip was cool, and she squeezed Christine's fingers.

"It's lovely to meet you," Christine said in a voice just above a whisper.

"It's great to meet you as well."

Roma's gaze swept over her, taking in everything, it seemed. Her lips twitched in a nervous smile and straight away, Christine fell in love.

She smoothed a hand over the skirt of her blue dress, knowing she looked her best with her hair done in cane rows that ended in a puff on top of her head.

Christine's eyes clung to Roma as she sat. Uncle Jimmy hung somewhere in the background, as did Auntie, but Christine couldn't look away from the woman she had imagined in so many dreams. If she blinked, maybe Roma would disappear.

It seemed she had waited for this moment forever, although it was only five months since she'd found out her real mother wasn't the one she'd known all along.

Roma's gaze still wouldn't settle anywhere for long and she fiddled with the lock on her purse.

Christine knew she was gawking, but couldn't stop herself from staring. Roma picked at her skirt, removing invisible things from the material. She raised her head and met Christine's stare. A slight smile lifted her lips before her gaze flitted away.

Christine didn't know what to make of this well-dressed lady, who wasn't saying anything, but that didn't prevent her from filling her eyes with the most fascinating person she had ever met.

"Ahem," Uncle Jimmy said.

That was Roma's cue to speak. "H-how are you, Christine?"

Christine leaned forward, not wanting to miss any words from Roma's mouth.

"I'm fine."

The room went silent. Roma raised a hand and smoothed her bun.

"I-I brought a gift for you," she said, gurgling as if someone was strangling her.

She held out a bag, which Christine took, making sure their fingers brushed.

Christine laid it on the cushion beside her. "Thanks."

Her eyes stayed glued to Roma, who shifted as though someone had flung a handful of pebbles in her seat.

"I have a gift for you too," Christine said, remembering the bag next to her. She stretched her hand to Roma, the handles of the bag resting on her fingers.

"Thank you," Roma said.

Their fingers brushed again as she took the gift bag. She opened it and a smile lit her face after she looked inside. Christine basked in Roma's approval, thinking she did resemble her mother a bit.

Then she frowned and leaned back, disturbed. Roma wouldn't look at her, not really, and she wasn't saying much. Christine guessed she didn't know what to say, and the questions she had bombarded Auntie with during the past few days disappeared. She couldn't think of one sentence, after months of wishing and hoping to meet her birth mother.

Christine's eyes smarted while Roma studied her, holding herself as still as the monument in the town square.

Forcing back tears, Christine met her mother's gaze and wondered what was going on in her mind.

Somehow, she had expected them to share hugs and kisses, instead of sitting in uncomfortable silence and exchanging curious stares. If she didn't say something soon, the visit would be over, without any of her questions answered. She couldn't let that happen, so she asked the first thing that came to mind.

"Where are your children?"

It was the wrong thing to ask. Roma's mouth opened, but nothing came out. She tried again, and this time her words fell between them. "They're at the hotel."

"Which hotel?" Christine jumped on that.

"The one we're staying at, the Seashell Resort."

They lapsed into a noiseless void again. Christine laced her fingers together. Roma picked at more invisible things on her skirt while Christine's disappointment formed a blob in her throat which refused to move, no matter how hard she swallowed. The silence between them grew even louder.

Pressing her lips together to prevent her chin from trembling, Christine played with the lace on her dress. She blinked and a tear fell between the thumb and index finger of one hand. She rubbed it into her palm and could have hugged Auntie when she cleared her throat and got to her feet. "It's a long way back to the hotel, so I guess you should get going."

Brother and sister got to their feet. Uncle Jimmy squeezed Christine's shoulder, and Roma shook her hand again and murmured something Christine didn't hear, but was too forlorn to care about.

At dinner, Christine sat in a cloud of disappointment, hearing nothing as Aunt Celia, Uncle Michael and Claude conversed around her. She moved only when someone asked her to pass a dish. By the end of the meal, she had rearranged the food on her plate, but hadn't eaten. Christine was grateful Aunt Celia didn't make a fuss over it.

Although she felt her heart had dropped and settled at the bottom of her feet, Christine kept Auntie company as usual, while she washed the dishes. After she finished clearing the table, Christine filled the time by scratching at the pattern on the countertop. She puckered her lips, seeing nothing but the back and forth movement of her hand. Auntie came and stood beside Christine, where she sat on a stool and continued tracing the curls and squiggles on the tile.

Auntie rested a hand on her shoulder. "I'm sure you know things don't always go as we want them to. This was a first meeting, so it's natural you'd both be a little uneasy with each other."

Christine continued to rub the counter as if she was alone in the room.

"Remember she'll be here for another two weeks and you'll see her again before she goes back home."

Christine let her finger trail the grout between the tiles.

"Give her a couple of days. I'll call and arrange another meeting," Auntie said, her voice wobbling.

Christine raised her head to look at Auntie, who turned away. Christine was sure Auntie wanted to cry too.

Auntie went back to the window and gripped the sink with both hands, but didn't say anything.

A lone tear splashed on the counter and Christine went still. She swiped at the tile where her tear landed and tried hard not to let any more escape.

Sniffling, she got up and shuffled out of the kitchen.

Chapter 29

"What's wrong?" Cass asked, looking up at Christine. The girls sat on the verandah of the children's home, their arms entwined. Cass' cheek rested against Christine's shoulder, and Jamielle sat on Christine's other side, sucking her thumb.

Christine shook her head before she spoke. "Nothing."

"So why d'you look so sad?"

"I'm all right." Christine smiled, pretending everything was okay.

"If you say so," Cass said.

Their visit had shifted to Sunday because of the meeting with Roma yesterday. Not that it was worth all she'd gone through to prepare for it, Christine thought.

Josh slid across the verandah on his knees, playing with a fire-engine Christine had bought from lunch money she'd saved.

Sam sat on the ledge of the verandah, kicking the air. So far, he hadn't said anything.

"So what else is happening?" Christine asked, tapping Jamielle's chin.

"Not much. We all right. School is okay and…" Cass stopped and eyed Christine. "Aunt Lisa and Uncle David came to visit Josh."

Christine's brain couldn't come up with faces for those names. "Aunt who?"

"Lisa," Cass said.

"Huh?" Christine frowned at her.

"They came on Thursday and played with Josh for a long time."

Cass continued to talk, but Christine's mind spun in circles around the aunt and uncle she'd never heard mentioned before today. She'd ask Auntie who they were. When Sam spoke, Christine put aside her thoughts. "What?"

"D'you know how Mommy's doing?" Sam asked.

"She was fine when I went to visit."

"When is she getting out?" he asked.

"I don't know. You have to ask Auntie," Christine said.

Although Ellie Simms wouldn't get custody of her, Christine didn't want to think about Ma'am being responsible for her brothers and sisters.

After she thought some more, she relaxed; Ma'am couldn't leave the asylum any time soon. She *had* killed their father. Sam either didn't realize or want to admit Ma'am would be away for a long time.

Auntie and the girls' house-mother joined them on the verandah. The minute Auntie sat in the varnished, wooden chair, Sam spoke. "Aunt Celia, when's our mother getting out of the 'sylum?"

"Not for a while."

Sam's voice climbed higher with the next question. "How long will we have to stay here?"

"It'll be a while," Celia said.

"And how long is a while, Auntie?"

Now Sam sounded miffed. Auntie shot a look from Sam to Christine. Christine shrugged, unsure of what was up with him.

Auntie's hand inched toward the crucifix and then fell to her lap. "It's hard to say. Until your mother is declared fit to take care of you, this will be your home. Plus, there's the fact that she killed your father."

"So how come Christine gets to live with you?"

Christine sat up straighter and stared at Sam. Although living with Auntie still made her guilty, it bothered her to have Sam put it into words.

"We went through this before, remember? At Aunt Icy's house?" Auntie's tone stayed even, but her face was hard to read. "Your father asked me to take care of your sister and I have to do that under the law."

Sam's lips twisted and he glared at Christine and Aunt Celia.

"And what about us?" His eyes filled, and before anyone moved, he ran across the lawn without waiting for an answer.

Christine's heart doubled its pace and her chest grew tight, squeezing the air out of her body. She didn't realize Sam felt that way and blamed herself for not noticing.

He sped toward a cluster of trees and when Christine blinked again, he'd scaled the trunk and disappeared among the leaves of a Blue Mango Tree.

They sat silent; even Josh was still, reminding Christine of the day Ma'am killed Daddy.

Cass tugged Christine's arm, her face solemn.

When Christine looked down, eyes overflowing, Cass whispered in her ear. "Don't feel bad. Sam just misses being at home with you."

Christine nodded, unable to speak. It made no sense chasing after him. He wouldn't want to talk now. Like her, Sam preferred to be alone when he was upset.

Christine and Auntie drove home without their usual conversation. The radio filled the gap with the oldies music Auntie liked to listen in the evenings.

When they parked, Christine grabbed Auntie's arm to stop her from leaving the car.

"Who are Auntie Lisa and Uncle David?"

"They're not related to us," Auntie said.

"Oh, I wondered because Cass told me they'd been to see Josh. Who are they exactly?"

"Well…" Aunt Celia began, but didn't continue speaking right away.

Christine's mind swung into gear. *I'm going to get a long explanation. Something's up.*

"You know that sometimes children get foster parents after they go to live in homes?"

Christine struggled not to say anything though she longed to interrupt. At the last moment, she nodded and wished Auntie would hurry up with the explanation.

"Well, this couple, Lisa and David are interested in being foster parents to Josh," Auntie said, "You understand what that means?"

Christine nodded a second time.

"But nothing can or will be done until your mother is in a position to decide. In the meantime….."

She's not my mother.

Christine slumped in the seat, but didn't hear another word as relief flooded through her.

It was bad enough losing their father, but to lose Josh would be too painful.

Sam's words came back to her, stirring guilt. She hoped Jamie, Cass and he knew that if she had a choice, she'd have stayed with them. Not that she minded living in Auntie's house, because Auntie understood her. Uncle Michael and Claude were okay and Christine felt safe with them.

She decided to talk to Sam in private on their next visit to see if she could do anything to help.

Christine came back to reality when her aunt shook her. "Are you hearing me?"

"Uh, yes, Auntie."

Auntie's head shake said she knew Christine hadn't heard whatever she'd tried to explain.

"Not to worry. I'm sure we'll talk about this again sometime," Auntie said.

Christine nodded, swung her legs out of the car and headed for her room.

She crashed in bed, chin on her folded arms, wondering what Roma was doing.

Probably having fun with her family that I don't fit into.

What did they look like? The brothers who didn't even know she existed. A weight fell on her when she recalled yesterday's disaster. Maybe, for the next visit, she should write the things she needed to find out from Roma. If she did that, she'd avoid wasting time staring at her and not saying anything.

After eleven years, Roma should have a few things to say to her. She didn't even get a hug. Was that too much to ask? Some mother she was.

Christine unfolded her cramped arms and rolled over on her back to eye the ceiling.

Aunt Celia had asked her to try to be fair and she would. She'd write the list of things to ask Roma, and then remind Auntie to arrange that other visit.

Two weeks would fly by in a jiffy, so she needed to get cracking. Roma Wint-Douglas wasn't going back to Canada without satisfying a chunk of Christine's curiosity.

The use of her mother's first name, if only in her thoughts, was satisfying. She'd been doing it for a while now. It was presumptuous, but nobody else knew about it, which made it kinda sneaky-cool.

Kids with a real home and real parents didn't know how lucky they were. She wished she had that; even one parent would do.

Sighing, she got up to search for pen and paper.

Chapter 30

Christine put her pen down and looked at what she'd written.

1. How could you leave your baby?
1. How could you bear to leave me?
2. Did you think about me at all?
3. What if I hadn't written? Would you have forgotten me forever?
4. What do you plan to do (about us)?
5. Does your family know anything about me?

Chin in hand, Christine nibbled at the nail on her little finger. Another question stayed just out of reach. An important one she tried hard to remember, but couldn't grab hold of just now. She rubbed her forehead, but the question didn't come. She gave up and closed the notebook, leaving out the edge of the sheet on which she'd written.

Feeling restless, she crossed the room and sat on the bed. She picked up the book she'd been reading earlier and then laid it aside. She wasn't in the mood. Her mind kept going to the meeting with her mother, which made her pray hard for a better visit next time.

Christine wandered around the room until her feet took her back to the desk. Her fingers brushed the notebook and she flipped it open. Nothing. The niggling question was no closer than it had been moments ago.

She drifted to the window and leaned on the windowsill, breathing in the scent that hung in the air. Someone was mowing grass. The lawn mower juddered as it stopped and started. She poked her head outside and sniffed the air, enjoying the warmth of the sun on her face. Being outdoors always made her feel better.

She'd get her things and sit in the backyard. Maybe she'd remember the other thing she wanted to ask.

Christine didn't hear Auntie crossing the lawn, but saw her yellow dress from the corners of her eyes. She edged over on the wooden bench to allow Auntie to sit.

"What's that you're doing?" Auntie asked.

"I've made a list. I'm reading it over."

"What kind of list?"

"Things I need to find out from my mother."

"Mind if I take a look?"

Christine handed her the sheet of paper, and Aunt Celia read it in a few seconds. "Are you sure you want to ask her everything? She may get upset."

Christine bunched her brows in a frown. "You really think she'd be mad?"

"Probably." Aunt Celia drew out the word. "If I were her, I wouldn't be comfortable talking about some of these things."

"But why not?"

"Because they'd bring up painful memories."

Christine gave that some thought. "My questions may bring back bad memories, but how else will *I* get answers?"

Auntie picked up Christine's hand and laced their fingers together. "Tell me what you'd like most from your mother."

Christine looked at her slippers and let her toes move over the grass in zigzag patterns. She tipped her head forward and whispered. "I want her to care."

Auntie leaned in to hear Christine's words.

"I want a mother," she said "'cause I've never had one. Not really."

Christine couldn't be sure, but something flashed in Auntie's eyes, as if she was in pain, but Christine figured she had to be mistaken.

They sat in silence, while the lawn mower sputtered in the distance, and the wind hissed through the leaves of the Mango tree.

A while passed before Auntie spoke, stroking the back of Christine's hand with her thumb. "You know things don't always work out the way we'd like, right?"

Christine nodded, poking out her lips.

"So we have to learn to cope, as best we can, with our circumstances," Auntie said.

Christine wiped her expression clean, but resentment bubbled inside her. All she knew was that Roma had better not disappoint her next time.

Auntie wiggled her fingers to get Christine's attention. "This is a confusing time for you, but the best thing to do is take each day as it comes and live with what it brings. I'll be right beside you to help, okay?"

Christine nodded again.

"You might not get the outcome you'd like, but you'll learn to be thankful for the good things that happen."

"You're saying I won't get all I want?" Christine asked, looking at Auntie.

Auntie nodded and squeezed her fingers. "Would it be the end of the world, Christine?"

Christine thought about the question and then shook her head. As much as she hated to admit it, if things didn't happen the way she wanted, she'd still be satisfied with meeting her birth mother.

The world hadn't ended with Daddy's death. She had believed it might, but somehow, her life had changed for better.

Knowing that, she could live with anything else that came her way.

Chapter 31

Christine's slight frown conveyed her doubt while she thought about Celia's question. Then, her mouth curved toward her chin. Seconds later, her eyes narrowed and a tentative smile seeped over her face.

This child, so much like her brother in temperament, made Celia's heart ache. She had to discuss her feelings with another adult. Michael would help her sift through the complications.

Having decided that, Celia relaxed and enticed Christine to continue their conversation in the kitchen. "Would you like some ice cream?" she asked.

"Of course. What are we waiting for?" Christine said, gathering her things.

Later in the evening, when the children were in their rooms, Celia shut her bedroom door and approached the bed, where her husband lay. "Michael, I need to talk to you."

Dragging his gaze from the television, he patted the spot beside him. "What's wrong?"

Celia got in bed and snuggled against his shoulder. "I'm just worried about the next time Roma and Christine meet. I want Roma to visit again, but don't know how to ensure that things go better."

She looked at the television screen while gathering her thoughts. "Christine made a list of questions I'm afraid will upset Roma. They don't have much time together and I want Christine to come away from this experience with something positive."

Michael squeezed Celia closer. "I hate to tell you, but it won't get any easier. Christine, determined little thing that she is, has waited five months for this. If I were in her position, I'd have a million things to ask too."

While he rubbed her arm in a comforting rhythm, Celia gazed at their legs, absorbing his words.

"As long as you know what her questions are going to be and you're fairly comfortable with them, I don't see the point in not letting her ask them. The way I see it, Roma owes it to Christine to help her understand why she made the choice she did."

He smiled and a mischievous light shone in his eyes. "What's the worst that can happen? One, she may refuse to answer Christine's questions and having agreed to meet, I don't think she'll do that. Two, she may run screaming from the room, at her daughter's audacity."

He broke out laughing at his joke. Celia poked him in the side, chuckling despite her concern. "Be serious, will you!"

"I tell you all the time. You worry too much. From the sound of things, Roma is riddled with guilt. She feels awkward and that's natural. Christine has all these expectations and romantic ideas she's pinned on Roma. After Ellie, who can blame her?"

He sighed and then continued, "She'll be disappointed to some extent. We have to face that, but it'll be a learning process for her. Life sometimes throws curve balls and we have to play catch as best we can. She'll get through it. She's tough and she has an awesome aunt who'll be there to help her, remember?"

He jostled Celia as he spoke, drawing a smile out of her despite her misgivings. "Okay, sir," she said. "I'll defer to your wisdom, although you're just an insurance salesman."

"You better. I'm the smart one. Remember you only have adult company for a tiny portion of each day."

They both laughed and Michael went back to watching television, with Celia nestled against his shoulder, working through her strategy.

She'd call Roma in the morning and level with her so she could prepare for Christine's questions. Things might go better if Roma knew what to expect.

What she told Christine was up to her, but she must have figured out by now her child was no fool and would see through any shilly-shallying.

Did Roma ever think this day would come? Maybe not. Living in another country would give her an illusion of safety, knowing she'd kept her secret tucked away on an island, thousands of miles from her immediate life. But even well-kept secrets had a way of jumping up to bite people when they least expected it.

Celia massaged her temples, shooing away the headache she felt coming on, and decided to go to bed. In the morning she'd be rested and better able to take care of any potential problems.

Chapter 32

Farther south on the island, Roma faced her own troubling thoughts. She dreaded falling asleep to risk encountering the demons she had battled alone for eleven years. The dream was always the same. As her eyelids dipped, heavy with sleep, she prayed she'd have a peaceful night's rest.

That was not to be.

She sat in a courtroom fitted with dark, wooden panelling. The judge wore a black robe, and scowled at her, his eyes fierce. To her left on a raised platform, sat a jury of twelve men and women. All of them were people she knew; friends, associates, neighbours and relatives. Each time they looked at her with loathing in their eyes, she quailed and sank lower in the seat.

She was on trial, the charge being endangerment of a minor. Her palms sweated and her head spun. The government attorney, tall and imposing, pierced her with accusing eyes each time he marched past the table where she sat. His words also accused and threatened. The lawyer listed her offences, making her sound like the worst kind of person.

Her gaze darted to the jurors, who stared at her with disgust. In desperation, she examined each face. Every one of them returned her stare, eyes cold, intense and frightening.

Panic held her in a grip so tight, she missed hearing the lawyer's arguments. He now asked the jurors to find her guilty of abandoning her baby; guilty of willful neglect and risking the life of her child.

Her breathing went shallow. Sweat poured from her brows and stung her eyes. She blinked the salt away to no avail as perspiration continued to pour from her skin. With the back of her arm, Roma swiped her forehead, scratching her skin with the linen material of her jacket. Her chest heaved, her fists knotted and her gaze darted back and forth as though seeking an unseen enemy.

The judge's voice boomed as he asked the foreman to stand. To Roma's ears, his words were slow and distorted. "How do you find the defendant, Roma Wint?"

If possible, her heart pulsed faster, as if it would jump from her chest. The foreman opened his mouth and for a moment, she heard nothing. All eyes in the room stabbed her, and after a delay the verdict hit her like a concrete block.

"Guilty!"

The word echoed off the walls of the clustered courtroom. *Guilty! Guilty! Guilty!*

Her eyes flew open and she shot upright, hands braced hard against the mattress.

"I'm sorry, I'm sorry."

Over and over she whispered the words, rubbing tears from her cheeks.

Her husband stirred beside her, but did not waken. She willed herself to stop moving, so as not to disturb him. She peeled her nightgown from her sweaty skin and lay down, knowing she wouldn't sleep for the rest of the night. The nightmare had occurred less frequently as time passed, but since Christine's letter, it was back each night in dizzying colour.

Although she had looked forward to the family reunion for at least a year, Roma avoided thinking about her daughter and the man she had left far in her past.

She'd been prepared to slip in and out of the island without them knowing. The reunion was in Montego Bay, far enough to avoid running into anyone from her hometown. A discreet inquiry to check on her daughter's well-being would have temporarily silenced Roma's guilt, but Jimmy's attendance at Maxwell's funeral ended her pipe dream.

When Jimmy turned up with Christine's letter, a confusing mixture of emotions had gripped Roma. She was terrified of being found out, and the ever-present shame over her inexcusable neglect ate at her every day.

She couldn't help being proud of Christine's letter—obviously the child was intelligent. After shock wore off, resignation stepped in, along with resentment.

Roma had convinced herself the day would never come when she'd be forced to face what she had done. Now that it had arrived, in a way, it was a relief.

She'd drafted a stilted reply to Celia, which did not convey any of the mental agony and anxiety she bore alone. She couldn't tell her husband. How would she explain the deception? What possible reason could she give for hiding a piece of her past—her daughter, no less—for eleven years?

Her feelings for Maxwell had lain unresolved for as many years. She had thought their love perfect, but the unthinkable happened and her life turned topsy-turvy, thanks to her straight-laced, judgmental parents.

They gave her one choice. Abortion was a sin and therefore out of the question, they told her. She'd have the baby and give it up for adoption. They even made the arrangements.

Roma's only rebellion, the crime of having a relationship with a man her parents didn't approve of, was crushed without much resistance. After that, Roma had only defied them once more.

Instead of giving up Christine for adoption, Roma gave her to Maxwell. She'd regretted her decision hundreds of times since, but didn't have the courage to do anything but follow the path laid out by her parents.

She turned her face away from Charles, and let her pillow absorb the hot tears seeping from her eyes.

What a mess she'd made of things. Her past had become the present, and demanded acknowledgement. What was she to do? Continue to see Christine in secret and pray she didn't ask for more? Or, should she at least show confidence in Charles by telling him about Christine and hope for his understanding and support? He wasn't narrow-minded, but how would she explain her silence over something this critical?

If only Maxwell hadn't died. She'd have been safe because Christine wouldn't have had a reason or the opportunity to contact her. Jesus, what to do?

Why hadn't she done the right thing? She should have stood on her own two feet and married Maxwell when he asked. Instead, she gave away her child, like an unwanted runt from a litter of puppies, and look at what had happened.

Christine was disappointed in her, and Roma didn't know what to do to help the little girl feel less slighted. Christine wanted more than

Roma could give. If she weren't married and didn't have a family, the situation would be simpler to handle.

Only the Lord knew how much longer she could stand the strain without falling apart.

Swamped by confusion, Roma did something she hadn't done in years. She went into the bathroom, knelt by the tub and prayed.

Chapter 33

Ellie no longer cared which day it was. She used the calendar by the bed to mark off the days, when she remembered. The medication kept her calm, but sometimes she felt dizzy and her heart kept racing. She didn't discuss her symptoms with the doctor or nurse because she couldn't be bothered.

She sat by the window, fitted with burglar bars, seeing nothing. She left the room only when necessary and spent the days in a fog of disappointment. Her gaze skimmed the sanitarium's well-kept gardens, but her thoughts roamed far away.

She missed her kids, but didn't wish to take care of them. Christine was good for that. Ellie didn't miss Maxwell so much because they had grown apart a long time ago, but their arguments gave her the attention she needed. When he was around, she had someone on whom she could take out her anger. Christine also served that purpose well.

Ellie accepted that her condition wasn't normal. She hadn't always been like this, but as far back as she could remember, she had trouble managing her emotions.

Playing second in line to Roma Wint and her child made her bitter and resentful as the years passed. Yes, she had her children and Maxwell, to an extent, but that wasn't enough to satisfy her.

Maxwell had never stopped loving Roma and transferred the adoration that should have been hers, as his wife, to Christine.

Maxwell had cheated her. She agreed to be a mother to Christine and a wife to him, but he never forgot Roma—even though she left him. Ellie had wasted so many years with him, thinking he'd grow to love her.

In the beginning he was affectionate, but somewhere along the way, Maxwell closed himself off, and she couldn't stand not being the most important person in his life. Roma had run out on him and yet he'd put her on a pedestal. Christine took second place, and the other children came after, leaving no room for Ellie.

If they had done the sensible thing and moved on, he wouldn't be dead and she wouldn't be sitting in this asylum.

Sighing, she focused on a yellow and green croton bush under the window. Considering what she'd done, the asylum couldn't release her in the near future and she didn't care.

Maybe she would have improved if she'd taken the medication Maxwell had made her get. In a fit of fury, she threw out the last set and refused to buy any more. He hadn't forced her to seek treatment after that, and their fights became more frequent.

The rap on the open door jarred her from her thoughts. It was the male attendant, which meant it was time to see the doctor. The man gestured to her and she got to her feet.

He escorted her out of the room and down the corridor, gripping her arm. The familiar passages led them outside and then into another building, connected by a covered walkway.

Dr. Morales instructed them to enter when the attendant knocked at the door.

Ellie started seeing him a week after she was admitted and knew he was adding up all she told him. At some point, he would decide whether she was mentally fit to go to court or if she would stay in the facility.

She sighed and sat down at Dr. Morales' invitation.

"How are you today, Ellie?"

"Fine, Doc."

She dredged up a smile, even as her mind continued to travel into the past. Dr. Morales' mouth moved and his bushy eyebrows wriggled behind his glasses like restless caterpillars. Soon, she lost track of his words.

Her gaze roamed the room and she frowned at the tail end of one of his sentences. "...haven't responded to therapy. I'll have to make a recommendation in the next few weeks."

At the end of their sessions, she always came away with gaps in the time. When she returned to her room, Ellie reflected on the session with Dr. Morales, but couldn't recall one thing they had discussed.

She examined the room, wondering what life would be like if she had to spend the rest of it in the sanitarium or in prison.

Though she should have been more concerned, Ellie couldn't work up the energy to care about the future. Still, she needed to put things in order, just in case.

She had to see Christine.

Chapter 34

Celia locked herself in her bedroom after breakfast, sat and flipped through the telephone directory. When she found the number for the hotel where Roma was staying, Celia dialled, and then waited for the operator to connect her to Roma's room.

"Hello, Roma?"

"Yes? Who is this?"

"It's Celia. I wanted to talk to you about Christine. It this a good time?"

"Sure. Go ahead."

"Christine was a little disappointed over your meeting and naturally wants to see you again."

Roma sighed. "Yes. It was awkward. I've been thinking about her too."

"I'm going to level with you. Christine has all these questions she wants to ask and I don't want you to come unprepared. Some of them are direct."

Roma breathed deeply before asking, "What does she want to know?"

"Why you left, how you could have left her, whether you've thought about her at all, stuff like that."

Roma's drew a sharp breath and when she spoke, Celia wondered if she should have met her in person instead.

"I…Celia, what am I going to do?" Roma asked, with an edge of panic to her voice.

It was Celia's turn to sigh.

"I can't tell you what to do, but would it help if we met somewhere, to talk? It might clear your head."

"Yes, yes, I'm sure that will help. Can you meet me this afternoon, say one-thirty?" Roma hesitated, then said, "We can't talk at the hotel."

"I understand." Celia said gently. "What about the coffee shop at the Town Centre Plaza, here in Hoopersville? You know where that is?"

"Yes," Roma said, "I'll get Jimmy to take me."

"Okay, later then."

Celia hung up, picturing Christine and Roma sitting opposite each other, tongue-tied and ill at ease.

She'd been mistaken to think Roma had it all together. That was just an illusion and based on their conversation, she was having anxious moments.

If only Christine knew. Things were so much simpler at her age. Roma had much at risk, and only God knew how she'd work through the situation.

All Celia could do was listen and hope Roma found a workable solution.

Chapter 35

Roma sat across from Celia, her hands wrapped around a coffee mug. Jimmy dropped her off moments before and the two women had placed their order. The café was quiet, with a few customers seated around the room. Roma stared at the glazed tabletop, fascinated by something that eluded Celia. She tugged at both shoulders of the collarless blouse she wore and went back to gazing at the table. Celia took a sip of coffee and waited for Roma to compose herself.

She licked her lips and sighed before sharing her thoughts. "After I left Maxwell and Christine, I was a total wreck. I held myself together long enough to finish what I had to do here and then I fell apart."

She stopped and rubbed her forehead. "Months passed before I felt fit enough to face school and all that went with it. I thought about my baby and Maxwell every day. He deserved so much better."

Her eyes pleaded for understanding.

"He was the ultimate gentleman, treated me like I was really special and then I—"

Her gaze flitted around the café, which was decorated in several shades of cream and yellow. Celia suspected Roma was trying not to break down in tears.

Seconds passed before Roma cleared her throat and continued. "When I handed Christine to Maxwell, he didn't lay blame or beg. He just stood there, looking as if his world had ended."

Roma sniffed and drank coffee before she continued sharing her thoughts. "It's not that I didn't care. I just—oh what's the use of making excuses?" She removed tissue from her handbag that rested on the seat, and dabbed her eyes. "There's no excuse for what I did."

She ran a finger around the edge of the cup, staring inside. In her other hand, Roma clutched the tissue while she spoke in a monotone.

"Once I settled in Canada, I acted as if everything was normal and got on with my life, like my parents expected."

The servers moved back and forth behind the counter, distracting Celia. Roma's whisper drew her attention back to the table. "I think about her all the time. I tried to forget, but I haven't."

In a swift movement, she gripped Celia's hands.

"I still don't know what I'm going to do." Roma lowered her gaze to the tabletop. "Actually, I do. The first thing I'll do is let Christine know I care."

Celia looked at Roma's hands covering hers. "Are you prepared to answer the questions she may ask?"

"I'm going to try. That's the best I can do. I don't want her to feel that I abandoned her and never spared her another thought." Roma sniffed hard and studied their joined hands. "I have nightmares. Almost every night I dream I'm on trial for abandoning her. The dreams stopped for a while, but they've come back."

Celia turned her hands over and gripped Roma's. "Don't distress yourself, just think about what you can do now. Christine is more than willing to meet you half way. She's thrilled to find her mother and only wants to know you care about her."

Their hands separated when Roma drew hers away to press the sides of her eyes. She looked away, a frown creasing her forehead. "That just leaves Charles. I want to tell him. It would be a burden off me."

She sat with her eyes closed for nearly a minute. Celia said nothing, giving Roma time to sort through her thoughts.

When Roma's eyelids flicked open, Celia gathered that she wasn't any closer to finding a solution to the problem, which urged her to speak.

"You've kept your secret for eleven years. And while it's been a heavy load to carry, I'd caution you against making any rash decisions you'll regret. Take time to think things through."

She took a sip of her coffee and met Roma's gaze. "I wondered why it was taking you so long to decide if you'd meet with Christine, but now that I think about it, you have your marriage and your family at stake. Again, I'd advise you to take a few more days to decide what you're going to do. Now is the best time, since you're all in the same place."

With one brow raised, Celia asked, "What kind of man is your husband? D'you think he'd understand?"

After considering the question, Roma nodded. "The only problem would be explaining why I've kept this a secret for so long."

When she smiled, it was more of a grimace. "Isn't it strange that after we make mistakes we see that the truth is always better?"

She smiled again. This time it was genuine, but marked by sadness.

"I convinced myself that since they were here and I was there, the truth would never come out. So much for that." Roma shook her head, before asking another question. "Tell me something. Was Maxwell happy?"

"No. Max was responsible to a fault and it cost him his life."

"I was shocked to hear he'd been murdered." Roma licked her lips before asking, "Where's his wife now?"

"At a sanitarium."

"Where are the other children?"

"In a home, where they'll stay indefinitely. It's unlikely that the authorities will release their mother."

Roma massaged the space between her eyes. "I know what-ifs don't matter, but sometimes I wonder if things would have been different if I'd stayed with Maxwell and raised Christine, not that I regret my marriage to Charles or having my two boys."

"I understand."

Roma spun the coffee in the bottom of the cup. "You'll think what I'm going to say is ridiculous, but I haven't been able to grieve Maxwell properly. It just wasn't possible.

"Christine is a different matter though. She's alive and very much a part of the present and deserves to have a relationship with me. She didn't create the challenges I face now. Maxwell and I created this problem. Maybe if he'd asked me to stay, things would be different, but he just let me leave."

Celia felt her back stiffening and opened her mouth to defend her brother, but Roma interrupted.

"Oh, who am I kidding? I made a choice. I walked away from Maxwell and our child."

Roma's thoughts took her away, and Celia chose not to disturb her. However, she felt lighter, as if a weight was lifted from her spirit. Christine's happiness had come to mean much to her in the short time she'd been entrusted with her care. Her niece had faced more hardship in her short childhood than she had in her forty-odd years. Christine deserved a break and it was time she got one.

Celia's cell phone trilled in her handbag. She pulled it out and answered. It was Christine.

"Auntie? The asylum called. They wanted to talk to you, but I took a message."

Christine's flat tone worried Celia. She squirmed in the seat and told herself to stay calm even as her heart pulsed faster. "Did they say it was urgent?"

"No. They just said to call as soon as possible."

"Okay, Sweet Pea. I'll be home shortly. I'll call when I get there."

Celia slipped the phone into her bag, wondering if something had happened to Ellie.

Chapter 36

Christine grumbled, trying to ignore the nerves that made her tummy rumble. It was bad enough she had to wait for another meeting with her mother, but now Ma'am—that witch—needed attention.

She sighed, hating when she got impatient because then she had nasty thoughts. She hoped nothing had gone wrong, like Ma'am hurting anybody else. That thought made Christine bite her lip hard and pray that something would happen to prevent her from seeing Ma'am again.

Auntie had promised she wouldn't have to visit unless it was important. The quicker Christine found out what was up with Ma'am, the better she would feel.

The moment she heard movement inside the house, Christine made a hasty trip to the living room. Each time it was Claude, going to and from the kitchen. That boy could certainly eat. After Christine scoured the rooms for the fifth time and peered out the front window for a glimpse of Auntie, her car pulled into the driveway.

Christine opened the door when Auntie reached for the handle. Before she could come in, Christine shoved a slip of paper at her. "Hi, Auntie. Here's the message."

"May I come inside?"

"Oh, sorry." Christine forced a laugh and stepped aside.

She took Auntie's hand and led her to the sofa near the phone, which rested on a side table.

"Have a seat, Auntie. Here's the phone."

Christine knew she had gone overboard, but couldn't make herself stop.

"Are you okay?" Aunt Celia asked, looking at her all funny.

"Yes Auntie, I'm fine. Go ahead and make the call."

Auntie picked up the receiver and dialled the number written on the paper. Then she raised one of her eyebrows. Christine understood what that meant and went to her room to stew until she found out if anything had happened to Ma'am.

The half-finished book on the desk didn't appeal to her, but she took it up and flopped into the chair. She bit her nails, hoping Auntie would come before she ate them all. After chewing the nails on her thumb and index fingers while her feet shook non-stop, Christine drew the chair over to the window and sat in it again.

The book rested face-down on her lap and she placed both elbows on her knees, cupping her cheeks. These days she was always waiting for something. Despite her nervousness, Christine giggled.

First, she didn't have much of a mother and now she had two of them. She hoped she was wrong and Ma'am didn't want her to visit again. She didn't want to go to the asylum last time and didn't want to go now. What if Ma'am tried to hurt her, especially since she'd never liked her anyway?

"Lord, please. Don't make me go back to that place. I'll behave myself," Christine whispered, thinking Auntie must have finished the call by now.

The breeze rustled the Palm trees outside, catching Christine's attention and slowing her galloping brain. She almost missed the knock at the door.

"Come in!" The high-pitched squeak that came out of her mouth startled her. She cleared her throat and called again, facing the doorway.

Auntie's face told Christine everything she needed to know.

She jerked out of the seat, and the book clunked to the floor. Ignoring the novel, Christine met Auntie's eyes, moving slowly because her feet had grown heavy as if someone had poured cement around them.

"Auntie, please don't make me go."

Auntie met her in the middle of the room and hugged her. "I wouldn't ask you to do this if it wasn't important."

"I know," Christine admitted after a moment and tipped her head back. "But what does she want this time? Why me?"

Auntie rubbed Christine's shoulder and cupped her face. "I didn't get to speak to her, but the administrator said Ellie has something important she wants to tell you. Remember their regulations prevent the younger ones from visiting."

"Will you stay with me like you promised me last time?"

Auntie nodded and didn't look away.

Christine lowered her head, so her voice was muffled. "I'm afraid of her."

"Hmm?" Auntie leaned away to see her better.

Christine repeated her words and then voiced her main concern. "She killed Daddy. How do I know she doesn't want to finish me off too?"

"I'll be there, okay?" Celia said, "I don't think she'd harm you. The medication is making her better, remember?"

Christine wasn't so sure about that.

Auntie took her hand and they walked to the bed, where they sat facing each other, their knees brushing.

"D'you think I'd allow Ellie to hurt you, Sweet Pea?"

Christine thought about it and shook her head. "She didn't do anything last time, so maybe I'll be okay. Just don't leave me alone with her."

"I won't," Auntie promised.

Shoulders slumped, Christine asked, "When do we have to go?"

"I figure it's best to get through it sooner, rather than later. How about tomorrow?"

"I guess," Christine said, as a familiar weight landed in her stomach and dragged it toward her feet.

Auntie stroked her cheek, which drew a smile out of Christine although she didn't feel the least bit happy.

"You're a special child, you know that?"

Auntie didn't wait for an answer, but gently pinched Christine's cheek and left her.

Christine sat with one leg curled up; the other hung over the side of the bed and her toes brushed the bedside mat. She squeezed her eyelids together while tears burned her eyes. Daddy used to pinch her cheek like that after they had a serious talk.

She hated thinking about Ma'am. When she did, she remembered Daddy and how much she missed him. Then she'd remember Ma'am had killed him, and didn't like how that made her feel. It made her wish that Ma'am was dead too.

Christine sighed; she was doing that a lot lately. Things were not going as she'd hoped, but mostly, they didn't anyway. She wanted more time with her birth mother, but wasn't sure how much she'd get and now the mother she had known forever suddenly wanted more of her time.

Life could be so confusing.

She got up and stood by the window, gazing outside. The breeze beat against the Palm fronds and it was almost as if they were waving to her, telling her everything would be all right. She hoped tomorrow would hurry up and get here and that she wouldn't have to stay long with Ma'am. Knowing her, she'd want something outrageous.

Chapter 37

Christine's heart tried to bang its way out of her chest as she ran. Ma'am chased her down a narrow, winding passage, shouting curse words. The belt cracked through the air, but didn't catch her. She ran faster. She had to get away…

Christine's eyes popped open and her mouth formed a silent scream. She'd had a bad dream. Her heart stopped jumping and she rolled over to squint at the clock. Six-thirty. Far too early to be awake.

She burrowed into the pillow, trying to steal more sleep, which didn't happen. She pictured Ma'am's room at the sanitarium and remembered how calm she'd been last time. Christine hoped this visit would go the same way, or better, since Ma'am was getting medication. Knowing Ma'am as she did though, Christine warned herself to expect just about anything.

The pictures flashing across the screen in her mind kept her awake. It was like living through a movie she hated, but couldn't stop watching, so she gave in and closed her eyes.

One evening, Christine went to bed without dinner because she'd spoken out of turn at the table. Daddy came home late and she didn't dare tell him about the cramps in her empty belly when he asked how she was doing. Ma'am's glare had silenced her.

She got little sleep because her tummy had growled the entire night. Sneaking into the kitchen wasn't an option. Fear of what Ma'am would do if she caught her stealing food, plus the creaking floorboards, held her prisoner in bed.

Christine shook off the memories, got up and went into the shower. It was better not to think about the mean things Ma'am had done to her. Not today when she had to see her, but her mind wouldn't cooperate and insisted on reliving the past.

She sat on the verandah of the old house hugging herself. Ma'am had told her to stay there although Christine protested it was Girl Guides day at school, which was why she came home late. Her skin remembered the stinging blows that came when she tried to explain.

"I don't care which day it is, you have no business bein' out this late," Ma'am yelled.

Christine's shoulders heaved as she cried, but Ma'am didn't care. She shook a finger in Christine's face. "Since you're old enough to be out at this hour, you're old enough to stay out all night."

It was five o'clock in the evening, which made Christine suspect Ma'am was upset because she hadn't been there to do her chores and look after the younger children.

The creeping darkness frightened Christine and she rocked back and forth in the chair she dragged into a corner. Cass and Jamie watched her from the window, but didn't dare come outside.

Christine trembled as the leaves rustled in a mad race across the yard, carried by the wind. Every shadow that moved sent fresh tremors of terror through her body.

Daddy found her curled up in the same spot when he got home after nine o'clock, hands wrapped around her knees, tears coursing down her cheeks.

"Christine, what are you doing out here?"

She hadn't answered and instead, hid her face. When Daddy raised her head, he knew. Hands shaking, he carried her inside and put her in bed. Daddy kissed her forehead, and turned away, his mouth curled in a scowl.

Soon after, the argument started. Daddy's voice came through the walls, muffled, but intense. Ma'am's words ran into each other and her querulous tone frightened Christine. Glass splintered and thuds sounded against the walls and wooden floor.

Cass and Jamie slept on, unaware of the drama being acted out by their parents. Christine was sure Sam heard them from his bedroom across the hall. As the bumps and loud talking continued, Christine prayed to God for forgiveness for wishing Ma'am would die, and stifled her sobs in her pillow.

The water stung Christine's skin, reminding her of where she was now. She shook her head to clear it of the bad memories because they only brought new fears with them.

She rubbed at the phantom pain in her upper arms from that run-in with Ma'am. Her belly rumbled and Christine dashed from the shower to the toilet, wishing again that Ma'am would forget about her or die and leave her alone.

Chapter 38

Celia looked at Christine, who slouched against the car door, sweating.

"Are you all right?" she asked.

Christine nodded, keeping her hands crossed over her tummy.

She'd ate little that morning and though concerned, Celia accepted Christine's explanation that she had an upset stomach and would throw up if she had more to eat.

She patted Christine's hands. "It'll be okay, you'll see."

Celia kept her eyes on the road, although concerned about Christine. Maybe it wasn't a good idea to take her to the asylum, but it sounded as if Ellie had information to share with Christine. Celia didn't know what it could be, and didn't want to ignore Ellie's request just in case it was important. Considering her situation, Celia hated to deny Ellie's wish.

When they got to the sanitarium, Celia rubbed her thumb over Christine's skin. "You ready?"

Christine made a fist and nodded.

Celia kept Christine's hand in hers from the parking lot to the reception area, and while walking to Ellie's room with an attendant. Celia squeezed Christine's fingers and smiled reassuringly before another attendant guided them through the open door.

Ellie turned from the window to face them, while the stout woman who had let them in squeaked away on the terrazzo tiles.

Ellie moved to the bed, allowing Celia to sit in the only seat. The female in white came back with another plastic chair. She offered it to Christine, who dragged it to Auntie's side and perched on the edge.

"What happen, Celia?" Ellie said, before her gaze swung to Christine. "You put on weight though, Christine."

"Yes, Ma'am," Christine said, not letting her eyes stray above Ma'am's waist.

"How are things?" Auntie asked.

"I'm all right. Hangin' in there."

"You wanted to see Christine?" Celia asked.

She wanted to get straight to business and make Christine's ordeal as short as possible.

"You never liked me, did you?" Ellie asked, cocking her head to one side.

Celia tried to hide her surprise, but didn't deny Ellie's statement. She glanced at Christine before she answered. Holding Ellie's gaze with her own, Celia directed her words at her niece.

"Christine, would you give us a minute?"

"Sure." Christine headed for the door, almost at a trot.

Celia glanced toward the doorway before responding to Ellie's jab. "Unfortunately, you and I have never seen eye to eye on anything, which is why I stayed away from your home. I was quite willing to accept you as Maxwell's wife and my sister-in-law, but you seemed to feel I had something against you. I want you to know I didn't."

Ellie broke their eye lock with a question. "How is Christine getting on?"

Though the sudden change of subject startled Celia, she didn't show it. "She's doing well, considering. Her grades are good. She's an exceptional child."

Ellie looked through the window and cut her eyes back to Celia after a moment. Looking past Celia, she spoke. "I did some terrible things to her."

Brows knitted, she scratched her neck. "I felt I had a right," she said. "Somethin', maybe jealousy, pushed me to hurt her."

She got up and walked to the grilled window, her cotton duster floating around her body. She had lost weight.

"As awful as it sounds, every time I hurt her, I got Maxwell's attention, even if it *was* negative.

"I'm not leaving here for a while, so I want her to understand that I didn't hate her, even when I thought I did. I hated the person I'd become, and took it out on her."

Ellie sighed and turned to face Celia.

"She had what I never had, what I craved. Maxwell's love. If only I'd stayed on the medication like he asked…

"I told her it was her fault, but it wasn't. I don' know why I killed Maxwell, but I did."

Ellie blinked once, twice, and then continued, "She must hate me, but I…" She frowned. "I wish I knew what's goin' to happen to my chil'ren. I can't take care of them. I just couldn't cope before. Christine did much better with them. I don' know why…"

She rubbed her temples, staring across the room.

Celia wondered how well the medication was doing its job. One moment Ellie sounded as clear as she used to years ago, and in the other her thoughts were all over the place and she was slurring her words.

"Can you understan' what I'm trying to say?"

Although perplexed by Ellie's behavior, Celia nodded.

"You must hate me for taking your brother from you. I know the two of you were close, but if you could try to forgive me…"

Celia didn't say anything, but watched Ellie circling the room and speaking as though conversing with herself.

Had she received any medication today? She must have, otherwise she'd have been more edgy. Celia wasn't used to this new Ellie. The Ellie she knew was resentful and antagonistic.

As Celia's mind wandered, she thought about the peculiar things that happened in life. If anybody had told her that within a week both Max's wife and his former girlfriend would make confessions to her, Celia would have said it was impossible. The reality said otherwise. The smile that came to her lips vanished at Ellie's next words.

"Would you give me a few moments alone with Christine?"

Celia swung her head back and forth before Ellie finished asking. "Why not?"

"She's scared of you, and I promised her it wouldn't happen. What is it you want to say to her that you can't say with me in the room?"

"I want to ask her to give a message to Sam, Cass, Jamie and Josh for me. I also want to tell her I'm sorry for the things I did to her."

Tears took a crooked path down Ellie's cheeks as she voiced her wish. Celia didn't trust her, even if she was saying all the right things.

"I can't say yes. It has to be Christine's decision."

"Will you try?" Ellie asked, tilting her upper body forward.

Celia felt Ellie willing her to do as she asked, but begging and hoping wouldn't make her wish a reality.

"I'll try," Celia said, standing.

At the door, she glanced back at Ellie, catching her in a triumphant smile. Celia stepped into the corridor, a shiver riding the back of her neck.

She shook off her discomfort, but decided to keep a close eye on Ellie just in case she tried anything.

Chapter 39

Christine leaned against the wall a little way down the passage. To her left, the aide who had escorted them to the room wheeled a trolley toward her. She was talking with a man in white, who Christine assumed was a nurse. She'd never seen a male one before now.

Christine turned away from the door, wondering what Auntie and Ma'am were discussing. She was curious, but just as happy being out of the room. She walked along the passage, praying she wouldn't have to go back inside.

At the end of the hallway, the space widened into a living area with comfortable chairs, a centre table and television.

The woman who sat inside the doorway acknowledged Christine with a smile. Christine assumed she was keeping an eye on the two patients who were watching television.

After a long while, Auntie called Christine's name. She turned and let her arms drop to her sides.

"Christine, sweetie, Ellie wants to talk to you now."

Christine's legs refused to move as if they had been glued to the floor, and if she didn't know better, she'd think a million mad ants were running over her scalp. Creepy. She ran her palms up and down her arms. "You won't leave me alone with her, will you?"

"As far as I can tell, she just wants you to give your brothers and sisters a message."

Christine's skin went cold, and her protest was loud in the silent passageway. "Auntie, no! She'll hurt me, just like she did Daddy."

"Come, hon." Auntie patted Christine's back. "Let's go talk to her together."

Christine stayed close to Auntie when they went back to Ma'am's room.

Ma'am leaned forward as if she expected something from Christine, which made her suspicious. Auntie had an arm around her, so Christine felt a jerky movement and could have sworn Auntie shook her head.

"Christine, come here," Ma'am said.

Christine looked up at Auntie, who squeezed her shoulder and tipped her head toward Ma'am. Christine's feet inched toward the bed, but she stopped where Ma'am couldn't reach her. She lowered her head, but watched Ma'am, just in case she tried to hit her.

Ma'am cleared her throat and folded both hands on her lap. "I've had time to think since I've been here." Ma'am coughed and made a sound in her throat again. "My head is much clearer since I started taking the medicine."

Ma'am smiled, something Christine couldn't remember ever seeing her do before today. She was downright scary. Christine stepped backward and hugged herself.

Ma'am stopped smiling and for a second, Christine thought she might start crying. "I wasn't a good mother. I have no excuse for that. I just hope you…"

She gazed at the window before speaking again. "You won' forgive me for taking your father away from you. I know that, but I hope you don' hate me too much."

Ellie stretched her hand as if she wanted Christine to take it.

Christine made slow circles on the tiles with her shoe and ignored Ma'am's gesture.

After a moment, Ma'am dropped her hand in her lap.

Christine's eyes flicked to Ma'am's face and darted away. Making an apology was the right thing for Ma'am to do, but Christine didn't trust her, not after everything that had happened. She edged away and when she bumped into Auntie, Christine slipped her hand into hers.

"Christine, I want to see you alone. Not for long," Ma'am said, sounding like she used to months ago, when she ordered Christine around.

The only sound was the voices that carried to them from the passage. Christine's sneaker prodded the floor harder. She stopped, took a deep breath, and squeezed Auntie's hand tighter. Auntie rubbed her thumb over the back of Christine's hand and returned her squeeze.

Looking Ma'am in the eyes, Christine shook her head, openly going against Ma'am's wishes for the first time.

Aunt Celia broke the silence. "Ellie, have you thought about asking for a supervised visit with the other kids?"

A smile brightened her face. "No. You think they'd allow it?"

"I'll make the request for you both here and at the home where they're staying. You never know, the answer might be yes. You haven't seen them in what, five months?"

Ellie nodded before she started pleading. "I still want to speak to you alone, Christine."

While Christine hung on to Auntie's hand, Ma'am looked at her aunt as if asking her to do something to make Christine obey.

"Let's go outside for a second," Auntie said.

Christine went past the attendant, who stood beside the door. Within seconds, Auntie followed Christine outside, drawing the door shut behind them. She held on to Christine's shoulders. "Sweet Pea, I don't understand what she has to say that is so important, but—"

"You know I'm scared of her."

Auntie raised Christine's chin with a gentle hand. "All I'm saying is that it might be easier to do it now. She's gonna keep pressing." Auntie smiled then. "And we might not get to leave at this rate."

Christine's stuck out her bottom lip and moved from one foot to the other. Her gaze swept up and down the corridor. Then she sighed and shrugged at the same time. "Oh, all right. If it will stop her going on and on about it."

She flung a glance at the door and whispered to Auntie. "Make sure you stay right here. I'm still afraid she'll do something."

"Okay, hon. I won't move a muscle, and remember the nurse will be with you."

Auntie pulled Christine to her and kissed her forehead.

"It'll be okay. You can do it," she said and gave Christine a gentle push.

Christine slipped back into the room. Although she left the door open, and the nurse stood close by, her belly gurgled as if she was going to have a bout of diarrhoea.

She stood within reach of the doorway, trying not to look as scared as she felt. The nurse nodded and smiled as if to say everything would turn out all right.

"I won' harm you," Ma'am said.

Christine's hand jerked and she pulled at her braids to cover her nervousness.

Ellie didn't move from where she sat, but pinned Christine with a steady gaze.

"Celia said something to me which makes me think you know I'm not your mother by blood."

Christine blinked like an owl and shuffled her feet.

"Like I said, I have no excuse for what I did. I just needed help." She looked at Christine as if waiting for her to say she understood. "I failed you and Maxwell when I broke the promise I made to him to take care of you. I'm really sorry."

Ma'am picked up a manilla envelope from the plastic fold-up table by the bed.

Christine took a jerky step backward. What if Ma'am had a knife? Gulping air, Christine slapped a hand to her chest and told herself to stop imagining the worst. A glance at the nurse reassured her she'd be safe.

"I want to give you something," Ma'am said, while searching the envelope.

When she found what she was looking for, she walked toward Christine, holding a white square of paper. "I found this a long time ago in Maxwell's things and I kept it."

She didn't meet Christine's eyes while handing over the envelope. "He probably didn't think you'd get this at eleven, but…"

Something slid inside in the envelope when Christine took it. Daddy had written her name on the front.

They had always joked that Daddy's handwriting looked as if someone had dropped a spider in ink and let it run across paper. The memory of their laughter made tears stab her eyes.

"Thank you," Christine said, sliding the envelope into the oversized pocket on the front of her jeans dress. When she raised her head and found Ma'am watching her, Christine moved farther away from the bed.

Ma'am got into bed, playing with a button on her dress. "Take care of your brothers and sisters, you hear? And tell them I miss them and that I love them very much."

Christine sniffed. "I will. See you."

She backed out of the room and barrelled into the corridor to hug Auntie's waist.

"I don't think I want to grow up for a while yet. Grownups are so confusing," she said.

Auntie patted Christine's back and then went to say goodbye to Ellie.

Christine turned the envelope over again and again, as if it was the most precious thing she had ever held in her hands, and it was.

Ma'am had taken whatever was inside without her father's permission. Christine was sure of it. She was dying to get home to see what was in the packet.

Chapter 40

Christine didn't wait for Aunt Celia to switch off the engine before she hopped out of the car and ran into the house. On the ride home, she'd swung the envelope back and forth, listening to the mysterious object sliding from one end to the other. She held it above her head, trying to see inside but didn't attempt to open it because she wanted to do that in private.

She closed the door, hurried to the desk and sat. Holding the envelope in one hand, she ran her index finger over her name printed on the white paper.

After she was satisfied with absorbing Daddy's handwriting, she turned over the envelope. Half the flap was unglued. Someone had been inside before her and she knew that someone was Ma'am.

Christine peeled back the flap, tilted one hand, and cupped the other under the packet. A gold chain with tiny links fell into her palm. A heart-shaped locket was attached, which she rubbed as she spun it around. One side felt a bit rough, so she squinted at it.

On the back, she made out the initials R.O.W. and when she looked closer, a clasp held both sides together. Christine flicked it open with her thumbnail. A much younger image of Roma Wint stared at her from the right side of the locket. The left side also had words engraved. Christine held the locket closer to see what was written there.

> *To: MS*
> *Love, R.*

At the thought of love between her mother and father, Christine's eyes burned and the chain and locket wobbled through the tears flooding her eyes. Sniffing, she put the locket aside and picked up the envelope. She removed a folded sheet of paper and held it open.

My darling Christine,

In the event that I'm not around to explain certain facts to you, I'm writing this to help you understand some of our family history.

I'm enclosing two things, a gift your true mother gave me years ago and a copy of your birth certificate, which will tell you your mother's identity.

Christine laid the letter aside and picked up the envelope, although she knew it was empty. Her nails raked across her forehead as she thought about the missing document. Curiosity overcame her worry and she lifted the letter again.

I didn't tell you Ellie isn't your birth mother because I thought it would make things easier for you, and for her.

If I had told you anything before the time was right, you wouldn't have understood. I hope I will have the chance to explain everything to you. In the event that I don't, I hope this explanation will help ease your mind.

Celia will tell you what you need to know, if you care to find out more about your mother. My sister will become your legal guardian if I should die while you're still a minor since the relationship between yourself and Ellie is not what I had hoped for.

There are things in my life I regret doing, as well as things I should have done and never did. I failed to create a better environment for you. That's because many things didn't work out the way I planned and I didn't do enough to change our situation.

I see so much of who I am reflected in you and hope you'll use every opportunity given to you and avoid making the same mistakes I did.

I hope you can forgive me.

Your loving father,

Maxwell

The letter fell from Christine's hand and she let her forehead rest on her folded arms. Fresh tears took her by surprise. She had started crying less since moving in with Auntie, but this new knowledge changed things. Violent sobs clawed her chest and pained her throat.

She cried because Ma'am had stolen Daddy's life and because she still didn't have a mother.

Minutes passed before Christine realized someone was rubbing her back, and without raising her head, knew it was Auntie. She hadn't heard the door open, nor did she know anyone could hear her crying.

Auntie pulled Christine to her feet, holding her close. The tears refused to stop and Christine wasn't sure how long they stood there, but Auntie held her until she had no tears left.

Auntie led Christine to the bathroom, where she rinsed her face and dried her skin. Then, she went back to her room and sat down at the desk, as blue as the day of Daddy's funeral.

When Auntie came into the bedroom, she brought a glass of water which Christine drank. Christine wasn't in the mood for talking, so she shoved the letter at Auntie.

She moved to the window to read closer to the light and when finished, she gave the sheet of paper to Christine. "D'you understand all that Max said?"

Christine nodded. "I think so. But I don't blame him. I know he loved me."

Aunt Celia nodded and patted Christine's arm.

"I know you love me too," Christine said, waving both hands to include the room. "You've done everything to make me fit in here, same as Daddy would have done for me."

"I have to admit I was a little afraid when you came to live with us."

"Afraid, Auntie? You?"

"Yes, Christine. Me." Auntie sat on the bed. "It's not easy raising a child. It's even harder when that child has just lost a parent she adores, and has been separated from what's left of her family."

Christine eyed Auntie, chin in hand.

"But you've coped so well, in so little time and under such trying circumstances," Auntie said. "I'm proud to be your aunt and I know Max would be proud of you."

Christine smiled, knowing Daddy would have loved her no matter what. "I'm glad I came to live with you, even though I still miss my brothers and sisters."

Auntie got up and went to the doorway. "I'm happy too. You're fast becoming the daughter I never had."

She smiled again before closing the door.

"I love you, Auntie," Christine whispered.

Facing the desk, she picked up the locket and studied the face in the picture. Although she wanted to get the next meeting over as soon as possible, it didn't matter as much as it did yesterday or the day before.

Auntie was the one who'd gone with her to the asylum today and would be with her the next time she saw Roma.

Holding the locket closer, Christine met the gaze of the woman who looked at her from the picture.

And when you go back to Canada, Auntie will still be here with me.

Christine snapped the locket shut and put it into the drawer, wondering where her birth certificate had gone and why.

Chapter 41

Christine bit her thumbnail and waited for someone to pick up the phone.

Jackie answered, sounding happy as always.

"Auntie set up the next meeting with my mother."

"Cool," Jackie drew the word into two long syllables. "When?"

"Tomorrow."

"Sweet. I bet you're looking forward to that."

"Well, I'm not as excited as I was the first time. She'll come here again, with Uncle Jimmy, like she's ashamed of me or something. Anyway, I just wanted to fill you in on what's happening."

"Okay. Remember we have to work on our Science project for next term and it's almost Christmas already."

"Gee, where does the time go? I'll remind Auntie that we have to go to the library this week. Catch you later."

"Okay. Say hi to Claude!"

Both girls broke into a chorus of giggles.

"I will. See ya."

Clutching her current read under one arm, Christine headed for the backyard. When she sat under the Mango tree, she opened the novel—one from the set Roma had sent her—but didn't start reading.

She squeezed her eyes shut, hoping Roma's trip wouldn't be a waste of time.

Christine hands dangled at her sides while Roma hugged her. So far, she hadn't yet acted like a mother, so Christine didn't get too hopeful this visit would work out any better. Like the last time, Auntie made sure Uncle Michael and Claude were out of the house.

"How are you?" Roma asked, letting her go.

"I'm fine, thanks. And you?" Christine asked, knowing it was the polite thing to do.

"I'm well, thanks," Roma said.

To Christine, Roma's smile seemed genuine and she didn't look as if she'd had a run-in with a ghost. That was an improvement over the first meeting. Still, Christine didn't get too optimistic.

Aunt Celia motioned to Roma and Uncle Jimmy to sit, but he excused himself and went to stand on the verandah with his cellular phone in hand.

To Christine, Roma seemed cheerful. If she was lucky, Roma would answer the questions she'd prepared. Christine decided not to waste time and started in as soon as Roma sat on the patterned couch. Christine sat opposite to both Auntie and Roma.

"Um, I have some things I need to ask," Christine said, moving to the edge of the cushion.

"Go ahead. I'll try my best to answer."

Christine unfolded the paper on which she'd written the questions.

"I wanted to know how you could leave me and Daddy," she whispered.

Roma cleared her throat and then sighed. "I didn't feel I had a choice. My family was migrating and I had to go with them."

Christine looked at her next question, but didn't have to ask it because Roma continued speaking.

"You won't believe me, but I've thought about you every day." She blinked several times before her gaze settled on Christine. "I figured you were fine. Maxwell adored you from the moment he saw you, so I had no doubt he'd take good care of you."

Christine told herself not to fall too hard for that story.

"What if I hadn't sent you those letters?" she asked.

"I guess I would have kept on thinking about you—"

"I don't understand." Christine moved her head from side to side. "You would have just thought about me forever?"

Christine went silent, staring at the paper. She was upset, but refused to cry. She breathed in hard and looked at Roma, who continued watching her.

"Didn't you wonder what I looked like? How I was? How my other mother was treating me?"

Aunt Celia spoke louder than her usual pitch. "Christine, give Roma a chance to answer, okay hon?"

Christine nodded, but while she studied her mother, her bottom lip edged out in a pout.

Roma raised a hand toward Christine. "I wondered about all that and I also wanted to know how you were doing. I wrote Maxwell once—"

Christine snorted, twisting the paper between her fingers, remembering Daddy's letter.

"Or twice," Roma added. Her chest rose and fell if she'd just finished sprinting. "Maxwell assured me you were doing fine. He never said—"

"What could he say?" Christine asked, keeping her voice even, "that my *mother* was abusing me. *You* left me. Daddy cared enough to be around to prevent…" She swallowed, unable to continue. "S'cuse me," she muttered before rushing from the room.

In the bedroom, she leaned against the door, drying her eyes on her shirtsleeve. Soon, there was a knock.

"Christine?"

Christine straightened up and opened the door.

"Are you all right?" Auntie asked, grasping Christine's arms.

Christine sighed, concentrating on the line between Auntie's eyes. "I'm fine."

"D'you want to come back or should I let them go?"

Christine sniffed and rubbed her eyes. "I'll come back."

Auntie linked arms with her and they walked to the living room.

"I'm sorry," Christine said and sat in the corner of the sofa, farther from Roma.

"I understand," Roma said. "I'd probably be asking the same questions if I were you."

She ran her hands over the cream skirt of her suit. After that, she smoothed her hair and fussed with the latch of the handbag on her lap.

CHRISTINE'S ODYSSEY ✢ 166

Christine rubbed at her stonewashed jeans. "D'you plan to stay in touch?" she asked.

"Yes, I do."

"How?" Christine demanded, looking straight at Roma.

"Well, we could exchange letters," Roma said, "and I could call you now and then. If Celia agrees, of course."

She glanced at Celia, who nodded.

Christine smiled and linked her fingers together, but she wasn't done yet. She edged forward to ask the next question. "Does your family know anything about me?"

Roma smoothed her skirt with both hands.

"I didn't think so," Christine mumbled.

"This whole situation is more complicated than a little girl can understand," Roma said. "I still have some time since we'll be here until after Christmas, so I'm sure I can work something out."

Christine shook her head and glanced through the open front door. Uncle Jimmy had walked to the gate, still talking on his cell phone. "I have to tell you, you and Uncle Jimmy are strange when it comes to family."

"What d'you mean?" Roma asked, pulling her eyebrows together and tipping her head toward Christine.

"Well, you both live in Canada and you both have children here."

Roma's mouth dropped open. When she got it to close, she frowned before asking, "What did you say?"

Christine repeated her words, slowly this time. "I said, you both have children here."

"I thought that's what I heard." Roma opened her bag, stared inside and closed it without removing a single thing. "How d'you know that?" she asked.

She didn't sound excited or anything, but Christine knew Roma was way more interested than she acted.

"Well, he took me to their house. I met Patricia, Simeon and their mother."

"I see," Roma said, tugging her ear.

"One more thing," Christine looked into her mother's eyes. "D'you have a copy of my birth certificate?"

It took her so long to answer, Christine wondered if Roma had forgotten the question, then she nodded and said yes.

"Would you send me a copy?"

"Yes," Roma said, "I'll send it with Jimmy, on his next trip."

"Thanks."

That was a relief, because Christine was sure she'd never get hold of the birth certificate that should have been in Daddy's letter. Only God and Ma'am knew what she'd done with it.

Christine wriggled until her back rested against the sofa. Although she smiled, she felt awful for pressing Roma so hard but didn't have a choice since adults had a way of avoiding questions they didn't want to answer.

She paid attention when Roma and Auntie started talking. Soon afterward, Roma and Uncle Jimmy left, having refused Auntie's offer of drinks.

Christine allowed Roma to hug her again and smiled when her mother patted her cheek because it was the reaction she expected.

Although she was far from satisfied with everything that happened today, Christine was grateful for two things—she didn't have to deal with Ma'am every day and she had a living, breathing mother of her own.

Chapter 42

Celia came back inside and found Christine sitting in the same position in which she'd left her. Roma had handled herself a little better on this visit, but Celia was sure brother and sister would have much to talk about after Christine's revelation.

She did well today, Celia thought. What a gift she'd been given.

She shook her head and smiled. Christine certainly dropped a bombshell on Roma. It seemed Christine wasn't the only skeleton in the Wint's family closet.

Christine's words stirred Celia from her thoughts.

"Auntie, was it my imagination or did my mother seem like she didn't know about Uncle Jimmy's children?"

Smiling, Celia said, "I don't think it was your imagination."

She refused to waste time insulting Christine's intelligence. Christine's next words confirmed the wisdom of that approach.

"Things at home might have been crazy, but at least none of us were treated like secrets our parents were ashamed of having."

Christine got up and strolled toward the passage. When she got there, she turned back to face Celia.

"You know what I'm wondering?" Christine's brows knitted in a frown. "If he has a family in Canada too."

Celia stared after Christine, thinking how astute she was for her age. Before Christine spoke, she'd been asking herself the same question.

Chapter 43

Roma dropped Christine's bomb in her brother's lap moments after the car pulled away from the sidewalk.

"Christine seems to think you have a family here on the island."

The car jerked side to side on the narrow road. Roma held on to the seat with both hands until Jimmy brought the vehicle under control.

"I'm sure she made a mistake."

Roma smirked. "So then, she imagined Patricia *and* Simeon *and* their mother."

Jimmy sighed and kept his attention on the road.

"So you've been keeping secrets, huh?"

"You're a fine one to talk," Jimmy said, casting a glance sideway at her.

"How can you make a comparison, Jimmy? I have a daughter. You've got a whole family stashed away, aside from the one you have in Canada. How on earth did that happen?" She held up a hand. "Wait, I don't want to know, but it does explain why you spend half your time here."

"Look at you getting all indignant," Jimmy said, eyebrows raised. "You've stolen off and probably told your husband you're meeting your girlfriends for lunch or something."

Roma ignored Jimmy's comment, which was accurate, as well as the heat creeping upward on her neck. She thought for a bit before speaking. "You're right. Who am I to judge? At least your children know their father's identity. Christine, on the other hand…"

She stared through the window, unable to find words to complete her thoughts.

"Does Julie know?" Roma asked, turning to eye Jimmy.

He answered after a while. "Yes and no. Patricia wasn't planned. She was born when we left all those years ago." Jimmy shrugged. "Considering how our parents think, what was I supposed to do? You know how they do go on."

"Yes, I know." Roma sighed. "But still, you should have done the right thing and acknowledged what you did."

"I told Jules up front about Pat, but, well…Simeon…Simeon came along after."

Roma slid him a disbelieving glance, but didn't press him for details.

"We've both made a fine mess of things, eh?"

"Yeah," Roma agreed. "Doesn't Julie worry about you being here so often, knowing the circumstances?"

"She used to, but she knows that it's business that takes me here."

"I bet she'd feel differently if she knew about Simeon."

"Anyway, this is not about my children, this is about Christine. What are *you* going to do?"

"I plan to tell Charles about Christine before we leave," she said, twisting the handle of her bag.

"More power to you." Jimmy let go of the wheel for a few seconds to pat her hand. "My secrets will remain just that—secrets. I can't face the upheaval I've seen since Max died. It's simpler to leave things as they are."

"Until they jump up and bite you in the butt one day," Roma said.

Jimmy sighed, but didn't answer.

Chapter 44

Christine scraped the last of the leftovers into the garbage and slipped the plate and fork into the sink, where Auntie stood washing dishes.

Hitching her toes on a rung of the stool, Christine swung onto the seat by the counter. "Jackie reminded me that we need to go to the library to do research for our Science project. You promised to take us, remember?"

"I forgot." Auntie turned off the pipe and dried her hands on a dishtowel. "I'll take you tomorrow. Is that okay?"

"Uh-huh, I'll call Jackie and let her know."

Christine went to the living room and rang Jackie's number. The Christmas tree in the corner reminded Christine how much she loved this time of year, even if they never had gifts like her friends at school got over the holidays.

Jackie answered in her usual chirpy tone.

"It's Christine. Auntie said she'll take us to the library tomorrow to finish up the research we have left."

"What time?"

"I forgot to ask. I suppose in the afternoon. I'll call you again in the morning, okay?"

"Yeah. How did the visit with your Mom go?"

"It went better than last time. I might see her again before she leaves."

"Cool," Jackie said, drawing out the word. "So, did you question her like you planned?"

"Yeah and maybe, and that's a big maybe, I'll even get to meet her family." Christine sighed into the mouthpiece. "That would be real nice."

"Yeah, that would be cool. So then you'd have what? A total of three brothers?"

"Four, including Sam and Josh. "I'm going to see *them* again in a couple of days. I hope Sam is feeling better. He cried last time."

"Maybe you should ask your Auntie if you can have them for Christmas dinner or something."

"You know what?" Christine's voice got louder with each word she spoke, but she couldn't help it. "That's a great idea. I'm gonna ask Auntie right now. Catch you later!"

"Bye, Christine," Jackie said, giggling over Christine's excitement.

Christine hurried to the kitchen, where Auntie was wiping the counters. The strong smell of bleach made Christine's nose wrinkle.

"Auntie, I have a question."

She looked up, holding the rag in the air.

"Um," Christine examined the swirls on the ceramic tiles to avoid looking at Auntie. "Would it be possible? I mean, can we…?"

Auntie dropped the cloth on the counter, moved to the sink and washed her hands. She came to Christine and tipped her chin up with her fingers. "What is it? Must be something big if my niece can't come up with a sentence."

Auntie's teasing loosened Christine's tongue. "I was just wondering whether we could have my brothers and sisters over for dinner on Christmas day."

"I'll have to ask permission from the home," Auntie said. "If it's fine with them, it'll be okay by Michael and me. Next time, don't be afraid to say what's on your mind, okay?"

"Yes! Thank you, Auntie, thank you." Christine hugged her, thinking her smile was in danger of splitting her face in half.

"Remind me to ask the administrator when we go next time," Auntie said, returning Christine's hug.

When they stepped away from each other, Auntie picked up the rag and went to the sink, while Christine made low whooping sounds and danced to music only she could hear. Doing that at home would have been out of the question.

Claude entered the kitchen and stopped when he saw Christine. He looked from her to Auntie.

Christine had never behaved that way before, but had little control over her feet and hands, which moved to a jerky rhythm.

"Claude," Christine sang, wanting to share her happiness. "Jackie said to tell you he-lloooo!"

His eyes brightened behind his thick lenses and he broke into a grin when Christine spun to the kitchen's entrance and sang a line from one of Rod Stewart's songs, arms held high as though she was on stage. "Auntie, have I told you lately that I love you?"

Auntie's broad smile made Christine blush. She sped away from the kitchen, unsure whether she wanted to giggle or continue singing. She entered her room and dove into bed, smiling at the ceiling.

I guess this is what it feels like to be happy.

Chapter 45

Christine yawned on her way across the living room to the kitchen. She'd woken up thirsty and after smacking her lips together and being unable go back to sleep, she decided to get a glass of water.

The phone buzzed as she went past, and she stared at it in the dark. Since she'd come to live here, this was the first time the phone rang so late. Clearing her throat, she answered. "Hello?"

A man spoke to her as if he was in a hurry. "May I speak with Mrs. Jennings?"

"Sure, hold a moment, please."

Auntie came on the line, having picked up the extension in her room. "It's okay Christine."

Christine hung up, but not before she heard the man say he was calling from the sanitarium. She stood over the phone as if she'd know what the call was about if she looked long and hard enough.

In the kitchen, she got the water she'd been on the way to drink when the phone rang. She took a glass from the cupboard, poured and drank the water, then returned the bottle to the refrigerator. After she put the glass in the sink and turned the light off, she went to the bathroom and threw up.

She had rinsed her mouth, used the toilet, and was back in bed when Auntie tapped at the door.

"Yes?" Christine sat up straight away.

The door opened and from the light in the passage, Christine saw that Auntie was dressed to go out.

"I have to go to the hospital," Auntie said. "Something's happened to Ellie. I'll talk to you when I come back. Try to get some rest, okay?"

"Okay." Christine hoped whatever had happened wouldn't force her to have to see Ma'am.

Auntie's car started up the moment Christine flung the sheet off her knees and ran to the bathroom. This time her bowels let loose.

Minutes later, she fell into bed sweating. What could have happened to put Ma'am in the hospital? Christine prayed again that whatever it was wouldn't mean another visit.

Even though her eyelids were heavy, she twisted and flopped under the sheet. Much later, she fell asleep.

When she woke, Auntie stood by the bedside, wearing the same clothes she'd had on when she left the house last night. She'd been watching her sleep.

Christine concentrated on Auntie's face while the pulled herself up to sit. Her twisting stomach said there was going to be bad news, even before Auntie started speaking.

She sat on the bed, facing Christine. More lines marked her skin than usual, probably because she hadn't been to sleep since late last night. She fiddled with the crucifix on her necklace.

"What's wrong?" Christine asked, hands pressed over her stomach. It was as if a monster she couldn't see was squeezing her tummy hard.

"Ellie had a heart attack last night. She didn't make it, Christine. She passed away."

Although Auntie had spoken softly, her voice sounded as if it came from a loudspeaker.

"How come?"

Auntie shrugged. "I don't know yet. The doctors aren't certain what caused it. Only an autopsy will tell for sure. They found something in her room. Medication that wasn't prescribed by the facility. Anyway…" Auntie's voice trailed away.

Christine didn't feel sad at all. She couldn't, but how would her brother and sisters take the news? Josh would be okay. He was too young to understand what was happening. Sam, Cass and Jamielle would be shocked and upset.

"Maybe she'll be happy," Christine said, still occupied with how she'd tell the others that Ma'am had died.

Auntie patted her hand and listened, while Christine voiced what she'd been thinking for a while. "She couldn't have been happy in that place even if the medication made her better."

"We'll have to go see your brothers and sisters later today to tell them," Aunt Celia said.

For the first time since their separation, Christine wished she didn't have to make the visit. How would she face them, knowing they had lost everything and things had gotten so much better for her?

Auntie stood, trying not to yawn.

Christine grabbed her hand. "Auntie, does it make me a bad person 'cause I'm not sad that she's gone?"

Auntie rubbed her eyes and sat again. "No, it doesn't. It's understandable because it's hard to sort out our feelings for someone who mistreats us. It's even more confusing when that person is a parent."

The birds chirped merrily in the garden as if sharing news with each other. They were the lucky ones, Christine thought. They didn't have a thing to worry them. She paid attention to Auntie when she shifted on the bed.

"The good thing is, she admitted she didn't treat you right. It's kind of hard to do, but it's best to try and forgive her. Don't worry too much about it. You're a good girl, and a blessing. Never doubt that."

Aunt Celia got up after patting her cheek. As she was about to close the door, she yawned again. "Do me a favour and make yourself some Corn Flakes or something. I'm going to get an hour's sleep."

Christine nodded and lay on her back, her head on the pillow. She let her gaze cruise the ceiling while she waited for something to happen. She blinked, but there were no tears. Scenes between Ma'am and herself played in her mind—the beatings and hurtful things she'd said.

Christine expected to be angry. Instead, there was nothing. She remembered Ma'am's last words to her. '*Take care of your brothers and sisters, you hear? And tell them I miss them and that I love them very much.*'

Did she know she was going to die? Thinking back, it had sounded like goodbye, but Christine figured that Ma'am knew she wouldn't be seeing the younger children for a while because of the asylum's rules.

Christine stared across the room at the window and prayed. "Dear God, please forgive me if I should feel sad 'cause somebody died and I really don't. Please take care of Sam, Cass, Jamielle and Josh. Help them not to be too sad. I ask in Jesus' name, Amen."

Then she got up to start the day. She rang Jackie and postponed their trip to the library. After she ate breakfast, Christine neatened up her room and tried to keep occupied until Auntie woke.

The book she was reading did nothing to take her mind off Ma'am's death or how the visit with her brothers and sisters would go.

Chapter 46

Christine fixed her gaze on the pictures of old-fashioned houses that hung on the cream walls.

They were at the children's home, where six of them sat in a stuffy room next to the Administrator's office. She had allowed them to use the space, once Auntie explained what had happened.

The room smelled of dust, which made Christine's nose itch. She figured that if she bounced in the couch, a dust cloud might rise from it and smother them. She shooed away those thoughts and looked at Sam, who sat at the other end of the couch. He wiped his eyes, refusing to look at anyone.

Cass blinked and moved her head from side to side, trying to stop her tears from escaping. When they ran down, she played with the hem of her skirt. Jamie sat close to her, like old times. Josh sat on Auntie's lap, playing with the crucifix on her necklace.

Auntie had told them their mother passed away the previous night. None of the children asked any questions. Christine thought her brothers and sisters probably felt battered and bewildered. It was hard losing Daddy because he'd been everybody's favourite, but it was so much harder for them, losing their mother on top of everything.

Sam startled everybody when he spoke. "So this means we have to stay here forever?"

"Well, at least until you're eighteen," Auntie said quietly.

Sam's eyes watered again and flooded his cheeks. Cass gave up trying not to cry, while Jamie stuck her thumb in her mouth and hid her face in Christine's shirt. Christine hugged her and stared at Josh's feet swinging back and forth against Auntie's skirt.

Christine shifted, uncomfortable with her good fortune. Her brothers and sisters had only each other, while she had a nice life with people she could consider mother and father.

Christine sighed and when she raised her head, Auntie shook hers. Christine understood that her aunt knew what was going on in her mind. Auntie's expression said that Christine hadn't caused this to happen and so it wasn't her fault. She'd had the same look on her face when she explained all of that on the drive to the home.

Nodding, Christine said, "I know, Auntie."

Auntie's raised eyebrows gave away her surprise. Smiling was out of the question, but Christine was pleased that she'd read Auntie so well.

Sam looked from Christine to Auntie and then at his knotted fingers. When Christine thought she couldn't bear the lack of noise and movement in the room, Auntie put Josh down and stood.

"I'll be back in a bit," she said, on her way to the door.

After she left, Sam cleared his throat and snorted to clear his nostrils. While studying his fingers, he spoke. "I didn't get to tell you last time, but I'm sorry."

"For what?" Christine asked, though she sort of knew what he meant.

"Blaming you for everything. I know you're not the reason why we're here," he said, wiping his eyes on his shirt sleeves.

"That's okay," Christine said, "I understand."

"At least *we're* together," Sam said, and threw his arm around Cass's shoulder. His smile was shaky and it took him a few more seconds to finish his thoughts. "You get to miss us. And apart from you and Auntie, Aunt Icy comes to see us sometimes."

Christine smiled and without knowing exactly what she was about to do, she stood. He met her halfway and they hugged. Cass and Jamielle joined them. Josh took advantage of the situation and climbed into the empty couch, lay down and sucked his thumb. That was how Auntie found them when she came back.

She waved for the children to come to her. "We have to go now."

She hugged and kissed each of them and gave Josh a big squeeze, which made him laugh loudly.

"We have to make arrangements for your mother's funeral, so we'll come back in a few days, okay?"

"Yes, Auntie," they chorused and filed out of the stuffy room.

Christine had to persuade Josh to leave the couch, by picking him up for a ride on her shoulders.

As always, they waved from the verandah. Christine latched her seatbelt and told them goodbye. She felt one hundred per cent better, knowing Sam wasn't angry anymore.

Closing her eyes, she blocked thoughts of the funeral from her mind. It stirred memories of Daddy's burial just months before, which still hurt too much to think about now.

She used the trick she had taught herself; for everything bad that happened to her, there was always something good. Her mother had promised to see her and there was still a chance she'd get to meet her other brothers.

She'd think about the good things in her life until it was time to face the funeral.

Chapter 47

While Christine and Jackie whispered to each other, the fan whirred over their heads, supplying background noise.

The interior of the library was cool and musty and the oblong table where they sat carried many scars, carved by children who had used the library long before them. Like soldiers on parade, the tables stood in parallel lines, and huge bookshelves dominated the other side of the room.

The fan lifted the edge of the page where Jackie's hand rested. Having finished their research, the only thing left was their regular chatting, not that they were supposed to be yakking inside the library, but that never stopped either of them.

"So, when's the funeral?" Jackie asked.

"We don't know yet. They have to examine her body before…before…"

"It's tough to lose your dad and then your used-to-be mom in such a short time." Jackie whispered and patted Christine's arm.

"Yeah," Christine agreed, "the only good thing, is that I may—"

"There's your Auntie," Jackie said, waving.

The pages lifted and flipped over, like an open accordion. Jackie grabbed the book and closed it, trying not to crease any of the pages. Christine gathered her notebooks, pens and pencils.

Both girls placed the reference books on the cart by the counter because only the librarian could replace them on the shelves. Then they rushed back to the table, crammed everything into their knapsacks, and hurried to where Auntie waited.

They told the librarian goodbye and left the building. Christine and Jackie sandwiched Auntie on the way to the car, reassuring her they'd finished their research.

Auntie treated them both to an ice cream cone, which reminded Christine of Daddy and the fact that she still had to deal with Ma'am's death.

Although it threatened to run over her fingers, Christine took her time licking the ice cream. Jackie chattered away with Auntie, but Christine was content to let her thoughts keep her company.

The funeral kept trying to push everything else out of her mind, but Christine shook her head, driving out the negative pictures. She turned the cone again, swiping it with her tongue.

Her eyes caught Auntie's and they shared a smile. She was so glad to have Auntie, who like Daddy, always listened to her.

While she crunched the cone, Christine's mind was in full gear. A couple of days had passed already and her mother had promised to see her again. She'd ask Auntie to see about that.

Chapter 48

Roma sat close to the plate glass, staring at the swimming pool outside their door. Shards of light danced across the water as the wind ruffled its surface. Though she enjoyed the water's movement, she shifted her gaze to avoid the glare. Her elbows rested on the glass-topped table and she shredded a napkin.

She jerked when Charles stepped out of the bathroom. She had forgotten he was in there. He came to sit across from her, covering her hand with one of his. "Want to tell me what's wrong?" he asked.

Roma examined his concerned brown eyes, neat moustache and his coffee-with-cream skin for a long time. Then, she looked at Charles' hand on top of hers and made a decision.

"I-I have to tell you something," she said. "Something I should have told you a long time ago."

"Sure. Go ahead. This sounds big."

When he smiled, Roma wondered how she had ever kept anything from him.

"I figured something was up when you sent to the boys off to the hotel's *Kiddie Kamp* for the afternoon, especially since we didn't have any plans that I knew about," he said.

He glanced at the bits of tissue littering the table. "You've not been yourself for a while."

Roma pulled away and cupped one hand under the lip of the table; the other, she used to sweep the pieces of tissue over the edge. She rolled them into a ball, which she dropped into the bin that stood near the wall.

Someone dashed past the door, and a splash followed. The teenager from the room next door had leapt into the shared pool.

She locked her fingers together and shot glances between the table and Charles' face.

"I have a daughter."

Charles' eyebrows met in a furrowed line.

Roma continued her story before she lost her courage. "I had her before we—my family and I—migrated to Canada."

She rushed on, trying to prevent him from interrupting her before she got to the end of her story. "Her father died. She wrote to me. I—I, we met. She's eleven."

Her hands, as though independent of her body, emptied the packets of sugar from the ceramic holder. They continued their work, putting them back inside. Roma couldn't have stopped what she was doing even if she tried.

"She—"

"Roma." Charles made her stop by gripping one of her wrists. "Look at me."

She met his eyes.

"I know," he said softly, but with some emphasis.

"You know?" she said, eyes popping.

He nodded.

"But how? And how long have you known?"

He drew a deep breath and his nostrils widened. "I've known something was wrong for a long time." He squinted at the pool and then met her eyes. "You get this faraway look at times. Actually, you've been doing it for years, and sometimes you're sad for no reason."

Her hands stirred, and she wanted to keep both them and her mind occupied, just in case anything bad was coming.

Charles stilled her hands with his and laid them flat on the table.

"I knew for sure within the last five to six months. You have nightmares and you talk in your sleep. You say things like, 'I didn't want to leave her', 'It's not my fault', 'Yes, I'm guilty', and sometimes you cry in your sleep."

"Why didn't you say something?" Roma asked, examining their hands instead of meeting his gaze.

"Why didn't you?" he asked, his question a gentle rebuke.

"I was afraid." Roma wiped away a tear. "You must think I'm an awful person for keeping something like this from you. I know it's dishonest, but it's been a secret for so long, I didn't know how to begin to explain."

Roma's stared into the past, where Charles couldn't see.

"Well, what I realize is that you didn't trust me enough to tell me," he said. "Am I so narrow-minded a person, that—"

"No," Roma shook her head and went back to filling and emptying the container.

"Then why did you find it necessary to keep your daughter a secret?"

"The truth is, these past few years I tried not to remember. Not to think about her too much. The whole thing was and is still too painful."

The table blurred and she abandoned the packets of condiments.

"I'm really sorry," she said, bringing both hands up to cover her mouth.

Her husband's face reflected her misery.

"I'm just disappointed you thought this was something you should manage on your own, that you couldn't trust me enough to share it with you," he said.

The minutes ticked by and Roma couldn't find words to explain why she had kept her secret for so long. She felt his gaze and moved her hands away from her trembling lips.

He shifted and sat back in the seat. "She lives here, right?"

Roma nodded and licked her lips, wondering what he would ask next

"And you've seen her since you arrived."

It was a statement that sounded like a question.

Roma nodded a second time, unable to bear the disappointment reflected in his eyes. She wanted to cry again.

"I want to meet her," he said.

Roma propped her elbows on the table, covered her face and sobbed into her hands. His willingness to meet Christine left her reeling and without words.

Charles let her cry, smoothing her hair until she stopped sobbing.

"What would I do without you?" she asked, when she could speak. He shrugged and smiled, but it wasn't a happy gesture.

"I dunno, maybe continue bearing your burdens alone, like you've been doing for so long," he said.

Roma got up and walked around the table. She touched Charles' cheeks and planted a kiss on his lips. "I love you," she said.

"I love you more," Charles said and returned her kiss. "We'll work this out, okay?"

She nodded, unable to speak because of the blockage in her throat. On her way into the glass and ceramic bathroom, Roma managed to smile.

In the small space, she examined herself in the mirror, taking stock of the tiny wrinkles around her eyes and the laughter lines bracketing her mouth. She had wasted so much time.

The next breath she took was the best and most refreshing she'd ever drawn. Her shoulders squared and to her own eyes, she seemed energized.

She laughed, realizing the weight she'd carried for so long had rolled away. She was light enough to float with the clouds.

"You're one of the luckiest women alive," she said to herself over the face basin.

Her lips tilted upward and she chuckled. Charles was going to love Christine. She was sure of it.

Chapter 49

"**A**untie, I'm *cautiously optimistic*," Christine said. Drama and mischief laced her voice. She laughed when Auntie did something she detested: she rolled her eyes.

Auntie didn't ask where she had picked up that phrase, but Christine could tell she was curious. She had been dying to use those words for some time and had now found the best opportunity.

They were in the car, heading for the resort, to see Christine's mother. Roma had called Auntie yesterday afternoon and invited them to come to the hotel. Christine had thought it excellent timing, since she had decided she wanted to have another talk with Roma.

Christmas was almost here and although Roma was going to be on the island until a few days after the holidays, Christine thought it best to see her the first chance she got.

Christine hugged herself. What a lovely Christmas this one would be, despite all that had happened. Her smile dimmed for a moment as she thought about Ma'am's funeral—one more thing to get through. With any luck, it would be before Christmas. If that was the case, she'd be free to enjoy the holidays without it clouding her mind.

She smoothed the floral sun-dress over her knees as the car drew up to the hotel's entrance. A uniformed man stepped out of the wooden guardhouse and approached the Suzuki. "Good afternoon, ma'am," he said.

"Good afternoon, we're here to see one of your guests. Mrs. Roma Douglas."

The guard made a note of their license plate number on the pad he carried, and asked for Auntie's name, which she told him. He wrote that down and then raised the metal bar and let them inside.

They followed the narrow driveway past the entrance of the hotel and around a corner that opened into a parking lot.

Auntie found a space, switched off the engine and smoothed her hair.

"Ready?" she asked.

Christine nodded and got out, swinging her beaded handbag that matched her slippers. Auntie locked up and they walked down the slight slope to the entrance. Christine slipped her hand into Auntie's, wondering about the name of the prickly bushes that lined the rock face on one side of the property. They entered the cool foyer and approached the desk.

A young woman wearing a colourful jacket stood behind the counter. "Welcome to the Seashell Resort. How may I help you?" she said.

"We're here to see Mrs. Roma Douglas," Auntie said. "She's one of your guests."

"Just a moment." The receptionist put the phone to her ear and pressed a few buttons on a pad below the lip of the counter.

Christine missed her words as she was busy eyeing the colourful, mini-tiles that decorated the counter. Something about them reminded her of summer and the sea. Her fingertips examined their contours while the woman spoke to Auntie.

"She'll be down in a few minutes." She pointed to a verandah, dotted with fan-shaped wicker chairs. "Why don't you both have a seat over there?"

"Thank you," Auntie said, taking Christine's hand.

They seated themselves near an indoor waterfall where blue-tinted water splashed from a stone fish with a gaping mouth. Christine sat on her hands and imitated the fish, which amused Auntie.

A shadow fell close to Christine and when she looked up and saw Roma watching them, her skin went hot. Roma appraised her with a slight smile, and Christine's gaze dropped to the bag in her lap.

Come on, stop acting like a baby, she told herself.

By the time Auntie and Roma said hello and turned their attention to her, Christine was her normal self again.

Roma wore a big smile. Her ankle-length, light blue dress swirled when she faced Christine. "All is well?"

"Yes, everything's okay."

"Wonderful." She turned back to Auntie. "Come with me."

Something was different about Roma today. It took Christine a moment to figure out what it was. Her eyes were dancing and she was smiling. For the first time since they met, Roma was happy.

Christine and Auntie followed her down a covered walkway, which led to another block of buildings. On their way, Christine enjoyed the cool breeze and splashes of red from the flowering Poinsettia that bloomed around Christmastime. She tipped her head back and looked out from under the roof. The sky was a wonderful blue with nearly transparent cotton candy clouds.

Roma hurried inside the next building and through a corridor with rooms on either side. She stopped at room 127, which had a silver doorstop holding the door open. Roma pushed it, calling as she entered. "Charles?"

"Out here," came the muffled response.

Through the gauzy material that covered the sliding glass door on the other side of the room, a tall shadow rose from a lounge chair. He met Roma at the door, wearing knee-length khaki shorts and a cream polo shirt.

Roma faced Auntie and Christine.

"This is my husband, Charles," she said, pointing to him and then to Auntie and Christine. "Charles, meet Christine and Celia."

Christine had yearned to meet her mother's family and not be a secret anymore, but was still shocked at being introduced to her mother's husband.

She did a rapid study. Mr. Douglas' eyes gleamed when he smiled. He was okay, right down to his coconut knees, which reminded her of Uncle Michael's pair.

She felt herself relax.

"So, you're Christine," he said, shaking her hand in a strong grip.

"Yes, I am." She grinned, giving him as firm a handshake as she could manage.

"It's good to meet you," he said. "I've heard a lot of nice things about you."

Christine felt him sizing her up, but couldn't help smiling.

He spoke in a loud whisper, pointing a thumb at Roma and tipping his head toward her. "You look like Roma. D'you get as crazy as she does, sometimes?"

Christine laughed and shook her head, while Auntie smiled.

"Charles, behave yourself," Roma said, chuckling at the same time. "Come, let's sit down."

They all sat in fat beige chairs, spread around a glass centre table in a tiny living area. Several door led to what Christine supposed were bedrooms.

"Anything to drink?" Roma asked.

"I'm okay, thanks," Aunt Celia said. "Christine?"

"No, I'm fine too," Christine said, laying her hands on top of the bag in her lap.

While the adults talked, Christine stared at the television screen. She should have been listening to the conversation, but her mind kept straying.

The corners of her mouth lifted into a smile without her permission. She wanted to hug herself. It felt great to no longer be something shameful her mother needed to hide. Tears burned their way across her eyeballs. She turned her head away and blinked a few times to clear her eyes.

When she turned her face back to the group, Auntie was watching her. She couldn't be sure, but thought Auntie nodded and gave her a smile meant for her alone. Christine smiled back and her eyes swam again. She'd have to be careful not to disgrace herself by crying when she had nothing to cry about.

She looked at Mr. Douglas while playing with the strap of her bag. He waved his hands while explaining something to Aunt Celia. Good thing he was a nice man; otherwise her mother wouldn't have been able to tell him she existed.

Just as she wondered about her missing brothers, someone knocked at the door.

"That will be the boys now," Roma said, "back from their hike on the nature trail."

She went to the door and while she spoke to someone standing outside, two boys raced into the room. Both of them looked like their father, but the smaller one reminded Christine of Roma.

"Hello," both boys said, coming to an abrupt stop at the sight of Auntie and Christine. The smaller one went to his father and squeezed into the seat beside him.

"Hello," Christine and Aunt Celia said.

The older boy took a seat on the opposite chair arm.

"Martin, Kevin," Roma said, when she came back into the room. "Remember I told you about Christine?"

They nodded and gave Christine sneaky glances, filled with curiosity. "Hi, Christine."

"Hey," Christine said, waving at them.

"Wanna see what we got at *Kiddie Kamp* yesterday?" Martin, the five-year-old, asked.

She almost missed what he had because his accent sounded funny, kind of like his father's. Christine nodded. "Sure."

They got up, and Christine followed them into another room, which was their bedroom. They showed her a set of miniature racing cars and Martin wasn't satisfied until she'd examined every one, which pleased him no end.

Roma came to get her when it was time to leave. "Christine, it's time to go."

She lay belly-down on the floor, between the two boys, helping Martin to colour a picture he'd insisted on tearing from an activity book.

"Okay, I'm coming." Christine dusted off her dress and got to her feet. As usual, time disappeared like magic when she was enjoying herself. She put on her slippers and in the sitting room, got her bag from the chair.

They said their goodbyes and Auntie thanked Roma and her husband for letting them visit.

Roma and the boys walked to the lobby with Auntie and Christine. On the way there, the two women had a conversation that didn't include Christine. She walked ahead with Martin and Kevin, chatting with them.

When they walked into the sunlight, Roma surprised Christine by pulling her close for a hug. Without saying a word, she turned and rushed back into the hotel. The boys trotted behind, trying to keep up with her.

Brows wrinkled, Christine watched Roma's blue dress floating on the breeze she stirred as she hurried away. Christine looked up at Auntie, but she didn't have any answers to the question Christine wanted to ask but didn't. All Auntie offered was a shrug.

On the drive out of the hotel property, Auntie slid Christine a sideway glance.

"Roma wants to spend more time with you before she leaves. She didn't get much of a chance today, with everybody there. Are you okay with that?"

"Sure," Christine said. "I suppose…"

She stopped, gazing at the blue-green waves of the Caribbean Sea on their right.

"What is it, hon?"

"I guess she wants to do that because she can't take me with her when she goes, huh?"

If Auntie answered, Christine didn't hear.

It doesn't matter, Christine thought, I only have one more thing I want to find out before she leaves.

Chapter 50

Christine pushed the striped yellow and white box away. Smiling chickens danced across the sides of the container.

"I'm stuffed," she said.

"Me too," Roma said, popping the last bit of chicken into her mouth.

She had collected Christine from home early that morning and they spent the day together. First, they went shopping. Christine had a wonderful time on the mall, trying on dresses and shoes, and was thrilled when her mother purchased the items she really liked.

They had also gone to the bookstore and left with a set of four mystery stories. From there, they went to the zoo.

Their outing was one Christine would remember for a long time. Before this, she had only gone on school trips and out with Auntie. She was gradually getting used to the Saturday morning 'girls only' trips with Auntie, but this counted as her first real mother-daughter shopping trip.

Across the table Roma smiled, and Christine truly felt her mother cared about her. She hoped that spending time together meant just that.

Christine hugged herself, smug in the fact that she was Roma's only daughter. When she thought about it some more, she squirmed because she was also Auntie's only daughter. Then her smile widened and Christine thought if she wasn't careful, it might split her face in two.

Boy, am I lucky or what? She was the only daughter to two really cool women.

"I had a great time," Roma said.

"Me too," Christine said, trying hard not to smile so much, but unable to make herself stop.

"It's a pity we won't get to do this again before I leave,' Roma said.

Christine's good mood slipped away.

Roma leaned across the table and gripped Christine's hand. "Don't worry. I'll make sure we see each other on Christmas day."

"I'd like that," Christine said. "I'm having my brothers and sisters over too and I'm looking forward to that."

"I understand. You only see them once every other week now, right?"

"Every week, when we can manage it," Christine said. She picked at her nails, trying to make a decision. "I'd like to ask you something."

"Sure."

Christine reached into the pocket of the jeans she wore. Her fingers snagged the item she'd stashed there and she lifted it out.

Roma gasped and took the locket, opening it to look at her photo. Gently, she caressed the engraving on the other side.

When she looked at Christine, her eyes were full. Christine watched, fascinated as the tears Roma tried to blink away ran down her cheeks instead. She opened her bag and was soon dabbing at her skin with a white handkerchief.

Unsure what to do, Christine patted Roma's hand. She wondered if she had done the right thing when more tears ran from her mother's eyes. Roma gripped Christine's hand tight. "Where did you get this?" she asked.

"My other—from Ma'am."

"It's okay." Roma encouraged her.

"She gave it to me," Christine said. "It was in a letter from Daddy. He told me about you and that my mother was not really my mother."

"So what you wanted to ask me has something to do with this?"

Christine nodded.

"When and why did you give it to him, considering what happened?"

"I gave it to him before I knew I was going to have you," Roma said softly. "And I gave it to him because I loved him."

Christine chewed over that bit of information. She looked up, challenging her mother. "Say all of this happened again, what would you do?"

Roma understood what she meant; Christine saw it in her eyes.

"I'd like to think I'd be stronger for my little girl," Roma said, brushing her hair back. "It's easy for me to see *now* how my life might have gone if I hadn't left, but things weren't so simple *then*."

Roma took Christine's hands. "Believe me, there's no way I would leave you again or forget about you now that you're back in my life."

Christine considered her mother's words, hoping she'd stick by them when she went back to Canada.

"You have Maxwell's fingers and though I see some resemblance to me, you look a lot like him," Roma said, letting go of Christine.

"Yeah." Christine sighed, remembering the old days. "Ma'am had a hard time with that."

Roma leaned forward and the look in her eyes scared Christine. Then, she stopped frowning and her face went back to normal. "If you need anything at all, I'll give it to you if I can.

"I-I can't take you with me," she said, "but as we get to know each other better, maybe one day you'll feel comfortable enough to visit me in Canada."

Christine's heart fluttered so hard she swore it was about to explode. She wanted to jump to her feet, dance about the restaurant and yell like a crazy person; instead she smiled wide enough to make her cheeks hurt and then said, "I'd like that."

Her next thought brought back reality. She fiddled with the empty chicken box and shivered. Suddenly, the air-conditioning inside the fast food outlet was too cold. "Would you do something for me?"

"I will if I can," Roma said, waiting for the question.

"Will you come to Ma'am's funeral with me?" Christine asked, her gaze fastened to the table. "I-I mean if you're here."

Roma didn't move for a bit and it seemed like a long time before she answered.

"Yes, I'll come if I'm here."

Christine slumped in her seat, her brain racing while she struggled not to grin. That was great. Getting through the funeral might not be so hard after all with Auntie and her mother there. She hoped they would hurry up and do the autopsy.

Her next thought wiped the smile away.

Things had turned around so much now that she had Auntie and Roma. Sam, Cass, Jamie and Josh needed a mother lots more than she did, and they had nobody.

Christine helped Roma put the napkins in the boxes and clear their table, wondering why everything had to be so complicated, even when they looked like they were going to be okay.

Chapter 51

Christine blinked, looked up and down and then gazed at the stained glass windows. She tried everything to avoid crying.

Sam jostled her on the way to his seat, further in the pew. He'd taken a while to finish the passage he read from the Bible and now plopped down and hid his face, sobbing into the sleeve of his grey jacket.

Cass and Jamielle hunched together, crying. Josh cried because all of them were crying. Christine hugged him and patted his shoulder. His sobs tugged at Christine's tears and she gave in and let them come although she wanted to be strong for everybody.

She cried, not for Ma'am, but for Daddy, whose funeral she had attended in the same church just over five months ago. She didn't feel bad about Ma'am's death, although anybody seeing her tears would think otherwise. That alone made her feel awful.

Christine scoured her memory and still couldn't remember Ma'am ever speaking encouraging words to her or saying she loved her. Every drop of love she'd received had come from Daddy and her brothers and sisters.

An arm rested on her shoulders and Christine remembered that Roma kept her promise and came to the funeral. Auntie pressed a handkerchief into Christine's hand from where she sat behind them with Uncle Michael and Claude.

Christine wiped her eyes, wishing Josh and everybody else would stop crying. The funeral was so much harder than she'd expected it to be. Thinking about other things wasn't working. She remained in the present, listening as her siblings sobbed and sniffled.

Why did this have to happen to them? No parents and no home. Life just wasn't fair.

As Roma's fruity perfume drifted into her nose, Christine thought about the important things that had happened up to now.

Yet, she wished their lives hadn't changed. She wanted Daddy back. Even if she'd never found Roma, she would have been content to have her family all together as they were months ago.

People moved to and fro, catching Christine's attention. The service was finished. As the funeral home attendants wheeled the casket ahead of them, Christine put her arms around Cass and Jamielle. Both girls had stopped crying, but their red eyes and trembling lips made Christine miserable. Aunt Celia picked up Josh, who rested his head on her shoulder. Sam walked with his head held down and Roma followed them.

In the churchyard, Christine remembered the fun she had with Roma days before on their outing. She examined each detail of that day while the pastor said the last prayer over Ma'am's grave.

The graveside songs tried to weave their way into her mind, but Christine focused on the conversation she'd had with her mother, who stood beside her.

Christine had seen the curiosity and recognition on the faces of some members of the congregation. Most of them knew Auntie, but Roma had them whispering and talking back and forth.

While she examined the grave, Christine forgot their neighbours. Some of the people there had to be Ma'am's relatives, but she didn't care enough to ask Auntie any questions. A few persons had sat in the front rows set aside for family, but Christine didn't know any of them. She was curious about Aunt Lisa and Uncle David, whom she still hadn't met, but was too gloomy to find out if they had come to the service.

The grave, sealed with cement, had four wreaths resting in the centre. People had brought many more arrangements for Daddy. Christine counted the flowers on the wreaths and followed the group of people with her eyes as they wandered away. Roma squeezed Christine's shoulder, which made her less miserable, and thankful.

It was over.

Christine approached the grave beside Ma'am's and looked around for Auntie. She was standing behind Christine and gave her the pink Calla Lilies she'd been holding. Before laying the arrangement down, Christine brushed dried leaves from the tiled grave.

She rested a hand on the headstone that held Daddy's name, date of birth, and death and whispered to him. "She came back, Daddy, and I think she actually cares."

Drying her eyes, Christine got up. Roma stood to one side of the grave, wearing a sad face. Christine left her there, just in case she wanted to say anything to Daddy.

While she stood waiting by the car with her brothers and sisters, Christine stared at her dusty shoes. They dissolved into a shimmering blur when her eyes filled again.

Auntie patted her shoulder, and Christine grabbed her around the waist and cried into her dress. She didn't understand why she was crying and didn't want to upset everybody again, so she let go of Auntie and got into the car. The others climbed in beside her.

On the way out of the church yard, Christine didn't look back. She'd see her mother again in the next few minutes.

Eyes closed, Christine laid her head on the back of the seat. By the time they got to Aunt Icy's house where everybody would gather, she'd probably be in a better mood to help cheer up her brothers and sisters.

Chapter 52

"So, now that Ma'am's gone, they'll have to stay in the home 'til they're grown up, right?" Christine asked.

Aunt Celia stopped digging around the roots of the Schefflera plants and wiped the back of her hand across her forehead, before she answered. "Yes."

"So who's their legal guardian now?"

"The state. Your mother didn't make a will."

"That's tough."

"Yes, it is. But you never know what might happen in the future."

"I guess it won't be so bad if they're together," Christine said, picking at a yellowed leaf.

"Family is important," Aunt Celia said, "and make almost any situation bearable."

"That's true," Christine said, nodding. She was about to start cleaning the yard when something occurred to her. "What's going to happen to our house?"

Auntie stopped turning over the soil and raised her head. "Max left the house and land for all of you, so it will be kept in trust until you're adults."

"Won't the house just get worse 'til then, since it's old now?"

"I'll have to look at fixing it up and leasing the land, so everything doesn't go to ruin."

"Okay." Christine collected dried leaves that had fallen from the Mango tree, dropping them in a heap, still thinking hard. "Did they find out what killed Ma'am?"

Auntie pushed back the brim on her straw hat and stood. "It seems she took medication that wasn't prescribed for her."

Christine frowned. "How'd she get it?"

"From what I gather, she asked one of her relatives to bring pills for her migraine, but what she got was heart medication instead. At least, that's what the autopsy showed. And by the way, you should never take medication that a doctor hasn't prescribed specifically for you."

"Gee," Christine said, "that's some medicine. Won't the person who gave it to her get in trouble?"

"Most likely." Auntie pulled her hat down and squatted again, tilling the soil. "But Ellie did take more than the recommended dosage."

"I see," Christine said, not seeing at all.

"It slowed her heart and eventually killed her before the attendant on duty found her. So it wasn't a heart attack as they said at first."

"I hope she didn't feel a lot of pain."

"I don't believe so."

"That's good," Christine said. "I hope she's happy wherever she is."

Christine waited a bit before she shared what else was on her mind. "I think she wanted to die."

Aunt Celia stopped sprinkling fertilizer and looked at her.

"What?" Christine raised her brows.

"Nothing."

"You look surprised," Christine said, "so I figure it had to be something I said."

"Uh-huh. You sounded so grown up just now. Why would you think Ellie wanted to die?"

Christine went back to picking up leaves. "Just something she said. It sounded a lot like goodbye to me. Maybe she took those pills deliberately. She had to be lonesome in that place."

"She definitely would have been lonely without her family. I hope she finds peace too," Aunt Celia said, gathering her tools. "Let's finish up and go inside. I'm gonna teach you how to draw Sorrel. Christmas is not Christmas unless we have Sorrel to drink."

"And Fruitcake! Ooh, only a few more days to go 'til Christmas. I can't wait!"

Chapter 53

"Remember you just ate, guys!" Aunt Celia called as Claude flew past Christine.

Sam chased him across the backyard, waving a life-like rubber lizard. Christine grinned when Claude yelped, moving faster than she'd ever seen him go. Plastic chairs scattered behind him.

He tripped and squealed, fending off Sam who shook the lizard in his face and collapsed, holding his belly while he laughed. The family laughed along with him.

Claude dusted off the seat of his shorts and let out a squeak, edging away from the still quivering lizard in Sam's hand.

"I'm not afraid of that!" he yelled, standing at a safe distance.

Sam found his next victim in Christine, who yelped and flung the lizard from where it had dropped on her lap.

"Give it a rest," she said, "It's Christmas. Be nice."

She muttered, shaking her head. "Dunno what I was thinking when I got you that thing."

Sam smirked and pocketed the offending lizard before he sat at the trestle table.

"Sorry," he said.

"It's Claude you should tell," Christine said.

While Sam laughed at Christine's grim tone, she hid a smile; she was thrilled to see him so happy.

She gazed around the backyard. Josh sat on Uncle Michael's lap, trying to steal his glasses. Cass and Jamielle sat cross-legged on the grass, playing with the dolls they had received in the family gift exchange, earlier in the day.

Auntie started clearing the two trestle tables of the leftovers from dinner, and Christine got up to help.

While washing the dishes, they watched everybody enjoying themselves through the window. When the cutlery, plates and glasses were clean, Auntie unwrapped two dark Fruitcakes. A large one with only a dash of rum and a smaller one, from which she cut two slices.

Six plates were loaded with cake, and rich, burgundy Sorrel poured over ice in a matching set of tumblers.

"Time for dessert," Auntie called, heading for the table in the yard.

Appreciative cries and groans filled the air while the children sampled the cake.

"This is delicious, Mommy," Claude said.

Auntie nodded and sat, while Uncle Michael cut a chunk from his Fruitcake.

Christine cleared her throat and spun in her seat. "Auntie, I have something to say."

"Go ahead." Auntie raised her eyebrows and put a fork-full of dessert into her mouth.

"I just want to tell you thanks for all of us." Christine let her gaze rest on Sam, Cass, Jamie and Josh. "You and Uncle Michael made this one of the best Christmases we've ever had. We wouldn't be together, here, if not for the two of you."

Sam and Cass nodded, unable to contribute anything with their mouths full.

Auntie breathed deeply, looked at Uncle Michael and held his hand before she spoke. "Uncle Michael and I have been thinking about your situation for a while. I know a couple visited the home a while back and were interested in being foster parents to Josh."

Christine's heartbeat pounded in her ears. The food she had eaten was heavy in her stomach. She put down her fork, eyes on Auntie who looked at each of them in turn.

"Michael, Claude and I—if you all agree—would like to have Josh live with us. We want to adopt him. He's the youngest and we want to make sure he stays with the family."

Christine heard nothing but the wind. Then she laughed and made a sound close to a scream. "Cool!"

When Sam and Cass slumped and looked at their hands in their laps, Auntie spoke quickly, spreading her arms. "If we could, we'd take all of you, but we can't so we're doing the next best thing."

She glanced at Christine before addressing the others. "Max and I have no other relatives, but we've made contact with a cousin of your mother's who seems okay and were looking at how best we can take care of all of you. I can't promise for sure that you'll be out of the home, but we're doing the very best we can to keep you together."

"How d'you feel about that?" Christine said to Sam in the uneasy silence.

"We'll miss Josh, but we'll see each other as we do now, right?" Sam asked, with an anxious glance at Auntie, who nodded.

"And you're saying we might get out of the home?" he asked.

Aunt Celia nodded again. "We're doing our very best."

Sam moved his head as though satisfied, while Christine stifled a smile because Sam tried not to look too pleased.

Everybody helped to clean up the backyard. Then they loaded the gifts into the car for the trip back to the home. When they were about to pull out of the driveway, a Honda rolled in with Roma sitting in the driver's seat.

Christine waved at her mother with a huge smile in place. Behind her, Sam craned his neck toward Roma.

"Who's that?" he asked. "She was at the funeral."

Celia got out of the car and motioned with her hands for them to do the same. The children climbed out and stood in the driveway.

"So who's she?" Sam asked in Christine's ear.

"My mother."

They gasped and stared at her bug-eyed.

"Your mother?" Sam and Cass asked in one voice. Their faces said Christine was mean to make that kind of joke.

"Uh-huh," Christine said, matter-of-factly.

"Well, are you going to tell us what's going on or not?" Sam whispered as they huddled together.

Christine glanced first at Uncle Michael and Claude who came to the door to see who had arrived and then at Auntie and Roma, who were talking to each other.

"Well," she began, "I found out, not long ago that our Mom wasn't my real mother. She kind of adopted me when she met Daddy."

Sam and Cass wore similar expressions; their eyebrows were puckered and they sucked their bottom lips.

"You mean you didn't come out of our Mommy's tummy like we did?" Jamie asked.

Christine, Sam and Cass looked at her, eyes round and brows raised. Christine wanted to find out how Jamie knew about things like that, but now wasn't the time to ask.

"Yes, that's it exactly, Jamie, but I *am* still your sister and don't you forget it." Christine tapped her nose, giggling. "Come on, let's go meet her."

Auntie introduced each child to Roma, who chatted with them for a few minutes. She had a special smile and a wink for Christine.

"She seems cool," Sam whispered to Christine.

"Yeah, she's all right."

"So how come she's been gone all this time and why didn't you say anything before?"

"It's a long, *long* story. I'll tell you next week. You know I can't come with you now, right?"

"Yeah, it's okay."

Cass and Jamie skipped past them and got into the car, with Sam trailing behind.

"Next week, guys!" Christine said while she flapped a hand at them.

Aunt Celia honked the horn, telling them she was ready to leave.

"Bye." Christine's siblings called in a single voice and returned her wave. Cass and Jamie made faces at her from the back seat. Christine rolled her eyes at their antics and caught Roma watching her, her lips turned up at the corners.

"I don't have to ask if you've enjoyed Christmas," Roma said when they sat on the verandah.

"It's been great," Christine said, "I got more books from Auntie and Uncle Michael and Sam and the others made me some cool stuff...and you're here..."

They exchanged a silly grin, leaning toward each other.

"I have a surprise for you," Roma said.

Christine's eyes went wide. "Really?"

"Yes, I do."

"Cool! Can I see it? What is it?"

"Well, I don't have it yet," Roma said, wearing a mischievous grin. "I had to get Celia and Michael's permission first. Now that they've said yes, Celia and I will make arrangements to get it for you before I leave."

"Oh, yeah?" Christine tried hard to sit still. "I wonder what *it* could be?"

"Let's take a ride and I'll explain why I'm getting *it* for you, before I tell you what *it* is," Roma said, winking.

"Oh, boy! The suspense is going to kill me."

"No, it won't. Just a few minutes and I'll tell you everything," Roma said. "Be a peach and go call your uncle."

"Okay, I just hope I can last," Christine said on her way inside.

Uncle Michael came out and while Roma explained where she was taking Christine, she tried to work out what she'd be getting.

In five minutes they were on their way. Christine bit her nails, still wondering what the mysterious gift could be.

Chapter 54

Roma drove into the parking lot at the botanical gardens and parked under the shade of a tamarind tree. She locked the car, took Christine's hand and they strolled along a cement walkway. Christine was surprised the garden was open on the holiday, until she realized from the sign that they'd opened in the early afternoon.

She was dying to know what the gardens had to do with her Christmas present, but forced herself not to ask any more questions. Her dad used to say 'good things come to those who wait'. While she waited, Christine considered the possibilities.

For countless minutes, they watched a group of ducks waddling in a line around the far side of the fenced pond. Christine was convinced she'd explode if she waited a moment longer.

"Um, I have to—"

"I know you're about to burst with impatience." Roma said, "Come, let's sit over here."

She pointed to a bench in the shade of a mammoth French Peanut tree. Christine wrinkled her nose at the smell of the blossoms while she waited for Roma to stop fiddling with the crushed-cotton skirt she wore. When she was done, she took Christine's hand.

"Now that we've found each other," Roma said, "I want you to be a part of my life and that means keeping in touch."

Christine nodded, fighting not to tell Roma to hurry up already.

"How much d'you know about computers?" Roma asked.

"There's a computer lab at school and we use the computers once or twice each week."

"Ah, so you do know how to use one."

Christine nodded, but couldn't stop squirming. This was better than anything she had imagined.

"Well, I want to buy one for you, so we can talk via the internet." Roma pressed Christine's fingers with hers, smiling. "Letters take a long time and I don't want you to forget me either."

Christine stared at Roma, her body going hot and then cold and hot again. "That's really cool. I can't wait to tell Jackie!"

"Jackie?"

"Yeah, my best friend from school."

They sat for a bit, enjoying the breeze and watching people strolling by their bench.

"Who named me?" Christine asked.

"Maxwell. Why?"

"Nothing, really. It's just that I've got a lot of things I'm curious about, but no answers. Now that I have someone to answer my questions, I hafta ask them."

"Mmm."

Christine tugged at her mother's hand, and Roma raised her brows when their eyes met.

"What were my grandparents like?" Christine asked.

"Are," Roma said.

"Huh?"

"You should have said 'what are'," Roma explained. "They're not dead."

"They're not?"

"No." Roma shook her head. "They're old fashioned. Strict. Straight-laced. But they've mellowed over the years. Our relationship will be a surprise to them. Speaking of which, do you know what we haven't done?"

"No." Christine moved her head from side to side.

"We haven't taken any pictures together since I got here. We'll have to fix that."

"That's true. A new picture of you would be sweet."

"There's one thing I must ask you," Roma said.

"What's that?"

"How d'you feel about me? Us? I guess I'm asking whether you'll let me try and make things up to you."

Christine eased her hand out of her mother's. The jeans skirt she wore wouldn't cooperate when she tried to make pleats in it. She licked her lips and then looked at Roma. "At first, I was dying to meet you. Then I was *very* angry with you."

Staring at the grass under her feet, Christine sighed, "Now, I guess I'm just happy that you—that I do have a mother. Ma'am and I didn't get along."

"Celia told me about your life before you lived with her." Roma touched Christine's shoulder. "I hope you'll be able to forgive me for leaving."

Christine rolled her eyes to keep from crying. Ma'am had asked her for forgiveness and now her mother was asking for the same thing. Adults sure seemed to do things backward, but Auntie was right when she said letting go of her anger would make things better.

Realizing that she had kept her mother waiting, Christine sniffled and sat up. "Okay, I will, but there's something else."

"Anything," Roma said, squeezing her shoulder.

"What do I call you?"

Roma smiled. "I realize that you never address me by any name. Let's see. You could call me Auntie, like you do Celia."

Roma squirmed and settled before she spoke again. "When you're ready, and only if you want to, you can call me 'Mom' as the boys do. I wouldn't mind." Her words ended in a whisper.

Christine hid a toothy grin and her delight. "Okay."

Side-by-side they sat in silence again until Roma spoke. "Time to go, Christine."

The drive back home went by too quickly for Christine. Roma and Auntie talked for a bit, and then Roma hugged Christine. Before they separated, Christine asked her mother to give Christmas greetings to Uncle Charles and her brothers.

Christine stood by the gate, waving until the rental car went around the corner. She hung on to the grillwork, thinking life couldn't get much better than the day she had just lived.

Chapter 55

As she had for the past couple of days, Christine sat mooning at the kitchen counter.

She dragged a spoon through the melting Pistachio ice cream, wondering what was happening to her. One moment she was happy and the next, miserable. Even Jackie had remarked on her moodiness, which was far worse than usual. She sighed and pushed the ice cream away.

Auntie stopped chopping vegetables, put the knife down and wiped her hands.

"Want to talk about it?" she asked, taking a seat across from Christine.

"I dunno," Christine said, cupping her face with one palm. Her elbow rested on the counter and she nibbled her nails.

"You remind me so much of Maxwell. He was just as moody sometimes," Aunt Celia said. "I'm worried about you. You're not eating much, or doing anything else. You sit around staring and that's not healthy."

Christine's chest heaved and her fingers tapped her temple. "I know, but she's gone and—"

"You don't think you'll ever see her again," Aunt Celia said.

Christine nodded and wondered why Auntie was trying not to smile.

"Sweet Pea, Remember you have the computer?"

Christine nodded a second time.

"Although she's thousands of miles away, your mother ensured that you have a way of reaching her whenever you feel the need.

Don't you think you mean enough to her that she will either come back one day or arrange for you to go visit her?"

Christine nodded but her usual sunny smile was hiding somewhere out of reach.

"And you have pictures don't you? Again, Roma made sure she took some before leaving and you both have copies. Isn't that something to be happy about?"

"I guess," Christine whispered.

"Plus!" Auntie put on a big smile. "We're gonna start the process of adopting Josh *and* remember we're doing all we can to get Sam, Cass and Jamie out of the home. It will take some doing, of course, but like I told you already, where there's a will, there's a way."

Christine tried to muster up a smile. "I get the point, Auntie."

"I sure hope so." Celia laughed. "And the point is?"

"I should stop being blue 'cause I have so much that is right in my life, huh?"

"If anybody ever tells me that you're not smart," Auntie said, wagging her finger, "I'm gonna wrap a frying pan around their neck!"

Christine laughed for the first time since she and Roma bid each other tearful goodbyes at the airport days ago.

"Auntie, that's funny. You're the best." Christine said, still laughing.

"No, Christine, you're the best. Come here and give me a hug."

Christine squeezed Auntie around the waist and made a face as she planted a big, sloppy kiss on her forehead. Despite her antics, Christine loved the attention.

"I guess I'll go check for mail or an instant message," Christine said, pouring melted ice cream down the sink.

"You do that," Auntie said and blew her a kiss that Christine caught and pretended to put in her pocket.

"Auntie, you know something?"

Auntie cocked her head. "What?"

"You're the best mother a girl could have."

Auntie went still, then her lips twitched for a bit.

"Thank you," she said.

Christine swore Auntie wanted to cry, but maybe she was wrong, 'cause now she was wearing the biggest smile Christine had ever seen on her.

Christine went to her room and crashed on the bed, eyeing the laptop on the desk. She folded both arms under her head and looked at the ceiling. The computer could wait a little.

It was time to think.

Aunt Celia was right. Life was good and the New Year promised to be better. Josh would soon be with them, which suited Christine just fine. Crossing her fingers, she prayed that Sam, Cass and Jamie would find a home just as she had.

She also said a quick prayer for her mother. There was so much to learn about her and Christine had the means to do it, thanks to the gift of the computer.

A smile sneaked up on her. She'd lost one mother, but gained another, two in fact. She still needed to get used to that.

Her mood shifted again and a sigh blew out from her lips as her eyes filled and her chest ached. If she'd stop crying so much, things would be perfect.

Daddy was gone, but she still remembered his 'pearls of wisdom' that he'd shared with her. Sometimes, he'd say 'out of every bad situation comes something good'.

For one moment, Christine thought she heard his soothing voice and smiled through her tears.

Life would never be the same without Daddy, but she'd found a place where she fit just right.

Saving Sam

Book 2 Simms Siblings Series

An insistent buzzing interrupted Sam's dream. His eyes popped open and he sat up straight, gripping both sides of the cot. His heart tripped with heavy, painful beats until he remembered he was safe at Downswell.

Leaning to one side, he slapped the Mickey Mouse alarm clock into silence and hopped out of bed. He slid his feet into flip-flops and picked up rag, soap and towel before hurrying to the door. A few boys stirred in the beds lined up on both sides of the dorm, but it would be a while before they woke.

In the shower, Sam rubbed bath gel over his body, spun under the stinging jets of water and got out fast.

He reentered the dorm with a towel wrapped tightly around his middle. Nine other boys, including Peter, his best friend, trudged past, half of them asleep on their feet.

Everybody rose early in the Downswell Place of Safety, where Sam had lived on and off for three years. During that time, he'd been placed in several foster homes. His last stay was with the Millers and he refused to discuss that five-month stint with anyone.

Since returning from the Millers' house, Sam was always first in and out of the showers. He never explained his need to be alone and no one asked. If anything, his housemother, Auntie B, was glad one of her charges was extra punctual.

Sam swiped both hands and feet with lotion and pulled on a pair of shorts and a tee-shirt. Then he opened the window and let in a blast of sunshine that hurt his eyes. His favourite tree beckoned from the middle of the lawn, but it was too early for him to seek refuge in its branches.

He made the bed, folded his pyjamas and placed them next to the pillow. After that, he grabbed the book he was reading from the floor, where he'd dropped it last night, and flopped into bed. Until it was time for inspection and breakfast, he needed to take his mind off things.

He opened the book, but instead of making sense, the words marched across the page like a trail of ants on a mission.

A picture of the house where he had lived in Sheaville, St. Elizabeth floated in front of him and a familiar seed of sadness took root inside him.

This slice of time during the early morning was one he disliked most. It allowed him too much time to think about the family he'd lost.

Life was better when his siblings lived in the orphanage, but Cass, Jamielle and Josh had moved out two years ago. Sam was the only one who hadn't found a home.

Tears blurred his eyes. He dropped the book on his chest, sniffed, and dragged a hand across his eyelids. If any of the boys caught him crying, they'd tease him for the rest of his life.

Don't be a baby, he told himself. He was better off than many orphans in Jamaica. Not all the homes were as clean and had good caretakers like Downswell. Auntie had said so after checking out several places when Daddy died.

He pulled out a photograph from the chest-of-drawers, peering at his father's smiling dark-chocolate face and the cluster of children around him. Even though Cass, Jamie, Josh and he had Maxwell Simms' complexion, Christine most resembled him. After his death, when the family split up, they found out why Christine had lighter skin and looked sort of different from the rest of them.

Their mother was missing from the picture, but that was fitting, because she was the reason Sam now lived in the home. The photo served as one of the few links to Daddy, but it was a terrible reminder that Sam was on his own. Auntie B's voice dragged him back into the room. "Ready boys?"

Sam swung his legs off the bed and joined the line near the doorway. He hadn't heard the boys return.

Auntie B was strict with them and before they filed out of the dorm each morning, she stood at the door, examining hair, nails and necks. She also smelled behind their ears, which they found hilarious.

"Laugh as much as you want," she'd say, "I just makin' sure all of yuh know how to take care of yuhselves when yuh leave dis place."

Short and round, Auntie B filled half the doorway. The boys in front of Sam got passing grades, squeezed past her and then it was his turn.

"G'mornin' Sam," Auntie B said when he stuck both hands out.

A feeble grin escaped him. "G'mornin."

"Yuh sleep okay?"

Sam nodded and widened his grin, trying to convince her that all was well. She peered at him, eyes narrowed, but said nothing further. Auntie B had not pressed him for any information since the first couple of times she tried to find out what was troubling him. After she completed the inspection, he escaped with a pat to the shoulder.

Breakfast was corn meal porridge and cheese sandwiches, served in the canteen where they had all their meals. Sam ate the sandwich and Peter devoured the porridge. As soon as their dishes were empty, Sam took them to the counter. Then he escaped to the room to make a list of things he needed.

Today was Saturday, which meant that Christine and Auntie were coming to see him. Each time they came, he got items he'd asked for during the previous visit. He tapped the pencil against his teeth, while deciding what to write. Although his appetite had not improved since his time with the Millers, he wrote 'snacks', which came in handy for bargaining in the dorm.

Auntie would bring shampoo, bath gel and deodorant. She never allowed what she called 'the essentials' to run out. Next, he scribbled socks and briefs. He'd ask if she would buy a new knapsack, because the one he had was falling apart. He folded the list and put it in the pocket of his shorts, and since he didn't want any company, he lay down and picked up the book.

While he'd lived at home, Sam hadn't cared much for reading and didn't read when he first came to the children's home. Cass, Jamie and Josh's leaving changed that. Reading had a twofold advantage; a book in front of his face kept others away when he wanted to miss his family in peace. The books also occupied his mind and took him away from the things he needed to forget.

He was engrossed in *Harry Potter and the Order of the Phoenix* when someone plucked it from his hands. Irritated, Sam hissed air through his teeth. Only one person would be so rude. He looked up at Ralph, the roommate he liked the least. Tall for his age, Ralph tended to be mean way too often.

"What you do that for?" Sam asked.

Ralph snorted. "Sun shinin' outside and yuh in here reading."

Sam grabbed at the book. "How that concern you?"

"Is what yuh reading anyhow?" Ralph held up the book, frowning. "Mus' be some sissy business. Jus' like you and yuh fancy words."

Sam rolled to his feet. "Gimmie my book!"

Ralph waved the novel out of reach. "What yuh gonna do, Sam, beat me up?"

"Gimmie my book!"

"And if I don't?"

Sam's fist shot into Ralph's eye and he doubled over squawking. Sam wasn't sure when he made the decision to hit Ralph. It just happened. Ralph barrelled toward Sam, who picked up the book off the floor and dodged.

He didn't move far enough.

Ralph's weight pushed Sam off balance and they fell across the narrow bed and dropped over the side. Sam hit the floor first, the breath squeezed out of him. His head banged the metal railings on the other bed and for a few seconds, his vision went blurry. He closed his eyes, willing the throbbing in his head to stop.

Something heavy pinned him to the floor. That load was Ralph, who whacked his cheek. Stars showered before Sam's eyes and he went blind again. He heaved upward to buck Ralph off his chest.

Ralph yelled in his face, but Sam couldn't make out the words. Feet thundered toward them as a group of children ran in from the yard.

"Fight! fight! fight!" the boys yelled.

Sam gasped and blinked a few times. The room rippled as if they were under water. Ralph was crushing him to death. Throwing his body forward, Sam knocked Ralph aside, then hung on to the side of the bed and hauled himself upright.

Ralph stumbled to his feet, chest heaving, eyes glinting with hate. Seeing the intense expression on Ralph's face and not knowing what else to do, Sam kicked him. The blow caught Ralph on the shin and he went down again.

Another wave of noise rose in the crowded room. Two boys hung on the grille attached to the window ledge and fisted the air.

"Fight! fight! fight!"

The refrain continued and grew louder by the second. The girls didn't add to the noise, but watched bug-eyed.

While Ralph huffed, Sam eyed him, but stayed out of his reach. Ralph lay on the floor, whimpering and hugging one leg.

A whistle blew and Sam's heart banged about as though trying to find an escape route. The room went so still, the shrill birdcalls from the yard ruled the silence.

The crowd parted to reveal Mrs. Brenda Reid, otherwise known as Brendasaurus, Chief Administrator of the Downswell Place of Safety. A frown covered her face and her lips were still pursed around the whistle.

Fighting was the one offense Brendasaurus hated more than any other.

Sam hung his head. Thanks to Ralph, he was in trouble.

Mrs. Reid blew into the whistle a second time. She stood over Ralph, hands on her hips. The whistle landed on her box-like bosom.

"What's happening here?"

Nobody moved or said anything.

"Sam?"

Mrs. Reid's voice rolled through his name like thunder over cloudy skies.

"Y-yes, Miss?"

"What happened here?"

Ralph yelled from the floor. "Sam punch mi in mi eye and kick mi!"

"Speak properly," Brendasaurus said, before turning to Sam. "Is this true?"

"Yes, but he grabbed my book."

Mrs. Reid pointed toward the doorway. "Both of you go to my office."

The wide-eyed spectators shuffled backward, giving Sam room to move. Ralph staggered to his feet and followed Sam, sniffling and snorting. Sam wanted to tell him to stop behaving like a pig, but didn't dare say a word.

"The rest of you, find something constructive to do," Mrs. Reid said.

The children left the room in a hurry as one body. Sam was sure the boys were glad to escape punishment for egging on a fight.

"Brendasaurus goin' kill yuh!" Ralph said, wiping his nose on the sleeve of his tee-shirt.

Sam glared at him. "Just shut up."

He knew better than to get into a fight. Why hadn't he done what everybody else did and just ignored Ralph?

Sam shivered and hugged himself, while wondering what Brendasaurus would do to them

Meet the Author

J.L. Campbell is an award-winning, Jamaican writer who pens romantic suspense, women's fiction and young adult novels. She is the author of thirteen novels, three novellas and two short story collections.

Visit her on the web at **http://jamaicankidlit.weebly.com** or **http://www.joylcampbell.com**.